CW01502043

DIRTY LITTLE
Lies

DIRTY LITTLE
Lies

CASSIE CROSS

Copyright © 2015 by Cassie Cross

No part of this publication may be reproduced, distributed or transmitted in any form or by any means, including photocopying, recording, or other electronic or mechanical methods, without the prior written permission of the publisher, except in the case of brief quotations for reviews or other noncommercial uses permitted by copyright law.

This is w work of fiction. Names, characters, places, and incidents are a product of the author's imagination. Locales and public names are sometimes used for atmospheric purposes. Any resemblance to actual people, living or dead, or to businesses, companies, events, institutions, or locales is completely coincidental.

Cover design by Mayhem Cover Creations
Interior Design and Formatting by:

www.emtippettsbookdesigns.com

For the latest news on upcoming releases, please visit

CassieCross.com

This book is part of *Dirty Little Series*. Reading *Dirty Little Secrets* prior to reading this book is recommended, but not required. It'll definitely help you understand the relationships better.

I hope you enjoy *Dirty Little Lies*!

CHAPTER
One

B en Williams is the mistake I will always regret, but will never stop making.

He and I have a long and storied history. We were the kind of tumultuous romance that makes for one hell of a cautionary tale. Together, we had a cyclical thing, and the cycle always begins something like this:

When I'm emotionally vulnerable, Ben shows up looking like sex on a stick, acting like I always hoped that he would. Caring, like he actually gives a shit about what's going on in my life. Loving, like he wants the two of us to be happy this time around.

I'm at a low point right now, so of course he knocks on my door out of the blue. This is the way things work between us. Or, it's the way things *worked* between us. I haven't seen Ben in nearly five years.

When I see him standing on the front porch of my brownstone, the surprise is overtaken by a quick wave of familiar desire. He's dressed casually, like he came over here on a whim. Low-slung jeans, a dark shirt, his hair tousled and messy, like he's been running his fingers through it all day. God, he looks good, and that is absolutely terrible news for me and my willpower.

Ever since Ben and I met, I've been attracted to him on a *cellular* level. I'm fine as long as we're apart, but the second we're in the same vicinity, every fiber of my being is drawn to him. Even now—even though we haven't spoken since I broke up with him for the last, devastating time—I feel the pull.

It's that pull that makes me open the door, even though I know I shouldn't.

I can't resist him. I've tried - it's impossible.

"Marisa," he breathes on an inhale, looking at me like he's surprised I'm standing right in front of him. Like I might not be real, like maybe he dreamed me up. "How are you?" His blue eyes are dark, and he speaks so softly, like he's worried he's going to scare me away. I haven't been a part of a gentle, kind conversation in a long time. It's that gentleness in his voice that makes me want to cry, and I've done such a good job of avoiding that lately. I'm certainly not going to allow myself to do it around him.

I've managed to keep it together for the most part since my family fell apart in the most scandalous, public way possible.

We're tabloid fodder; papers with our names and faces on them are everywhere. The destruction and downfall of the Blake dynasty is impossible to miss in this city. Some people are delighting in it, and I don't blame them.

Turns out that my mother and father—the illustrious Gloria and James—aren't the people that my sister and I thought they were. They're exactly who the Feds thought they were, though, given the incredibly damning case they've built up against Mom and Dad, details of which are all over the evening news these days.

That's why Ben is here, I'm sure of it. This is what he does: he shows up when I'm feeling low, and somehow manages to leave me feeling even lower. Still, he's one of a very few friends—past or present—who has contacted me since this scandal broke, so I'm reluctant to send him away.

Plus, that whole can't-resist-him thing is still in play here.

So, Ben wants to know how I'm doing? "Not well," I tell him.

He holds out a bottle of my favorite wine and says, "I was going to wait until the Murphy benefit to talk to you, but I read something this morning that made me think that I shouldn't wait."

I let out a short little sigh of relief, glad that he decided not to rehash whatever terrible thing he read about my family this morning that made him think that he needed to check in on me. The very last thing I want to hear about tonight is my parents. At this point, I feel like I could do without hearing about them ever again.

"Do you want to talk about it?" Ben asks.

I shake my head. I don't want to talk about it, especially not with him. Besides, talking? That's not what Ben and I do. We fuck, and then I try to turn that into some kind of a relationship. I give it my all, but he inevitably cheats on me, and breaks my heart. Then he begs me for forgiveness, and asks for another chance. Like a fool, I always give him one.

Always *gave* him one.

I've learned my lesson, and now I'm smart enough to know that I can only rely on Ben for mind-blowing orgasms. He's amazing in bed. Out of it? Not so much. Whenever I expect or hope for anything more from him, I get my heart broken, and I can't handle any more heartbreak right now. His body was the only thing that he ever freely gave to me, and sex with him had been almost...*transcendent*. Ben always used sex to make me feel better, so there's no doubt in my mind that's what he's here for tonight. There's no use in trying for anything more when that only ever ends badly for me.

So, I decide to take the few hours of bliss that Ben is offering to me, and leave it at that.

I invite him inside, push myself up onto my tiptoes, and kiss him.

We melt into each other, like always. Like it's been hours since we were together like this, not years.

Ben lets me get lost in the warmth of his body against mine, his lips on my lips, and his tongue, wet and warm in my mouth. He trails messy kisses along the column of my neck as he tears off my blouse. He cups my breasts, pinching my nipples the way that I like, the way only he can do it.

He drops to his knees and rucks up my skirt, bunching the fabric between his fingers. He presses short, sweet kisses along the inside of my thighs, then he slides my panties to the side and puts his tongue right where I want it. He licks and sucks and touches me, like making me come with his mouth is his life's ambition. I twist my fingers in his hair as I writhe with pleasure, his name falling from my lips.

With my hands curled around Ben's collar, I pull him up, kissing myself off of him. I take off his shirt first, then his pants. I already know all the places I need to touch, to kiss, to lick to get him going, so my hands and mouth explore every inch of him, until he's begging me for more.

I guide Ben to my bedroom and we tumble onto the bed, naked and wanting, as I climb on top of his body. With my knees planted on either side of his hips, I sink down onto him. For the first time in weeks, it feels like I can actually breathe again.

Ben fucks me like there aren't five years and countless breakups between us, and for a few hours, he makes me forget that my world is falling apart.

After, he lies naked atop my rumpled Egyptian cotton

sheets, tenderly pushing a strand of hair behind my ear. He looks happy, like everything is as it should be. Like he knows he's opened a door with me, and he's ready to step back inside.

Years ago, I would let him in. I would be so desperate for him that I'd overlook the cheating, and the carelessness, and I would fool myself into believing that it would be different this time. That I could love him enough to make him different, that there was something about me that would make him want to change, that he'd love me enough to actually do it.

I could cry for the naive, hopeful, lovesick idiot that I used to be with him. This? Tonight? It was just sex. That's all I ever was to Ben, and that's all he is to me tonight.

"I've missed you," he tells me.

I can't say it back, so I press my lips together to keep myself from doing something completely stupid. I could tell him that I've missed this—the intimacy that we shared, the physicality between us—but I don't. I could tell him that I'm glad he stopped by, but then he would think that was an invitation for him to do it again. I can't let myself travel back down that road, so the less I see of him, the better off I'll be. In fact, the best thing he could do for me right now is to walk out my front door and never come back.

Somehow, I know that won't happen, though. He'll come back, and I'll deal with that when it happens.

"Do you want me to stay?" he asks.

It would be tempting to let myself spend the night in his

arms, to fall asleep wrapped in the warmth of his embrace, especially since I've been feeling so lonely these past few weeks. Instead, I tell him a half lie, half truth.

"No. I don't."

"Are you sure?"

God, he's so beautiful up close like this. I had forgotten how beautiful Ben is. I had *made* myself forget it.

"Yes, I'm sure."

He sighs, and hesitates, but he doesn't argue with me like he would have years ago. He just slides out of my bed, giving me one last moment to appreciate his gorgeous ass before he pulls his pants back on. Once he's dressed, he walks over to my side of the bed, leans over and gives me a kiss.

In the end, he leaves just like he always does.

With us, nothing ever changes.

CHAPTER
Two

"**M**iss Blake! Miss Blake!"

A sea of reporters is lying in wait for me outside of my lawyer's office. They're swarming around the door to the building, holding up microphones and tape recorders, shoving cameras in my face.

I've been preparing myself for this all morning, ever since I looked out the window during a break in our meeting, and saw them all gathering outside. Till now, apart from the few reporters who have managed to find me at home, or on my walk to and from the coffee shop in the morning, I've managed to avoid this.

The questions, the hounding.

Before we stepped out of the elevator, my lawyer, Nancy, took my hands in hers. She asked me if I was ready for this. I told her I was, but it was a lie. I was nowhere near ready for this.

The flashes are blinding, even in the broad daylight, and the sheer number of people calling my name makes it difficult not to try to look everywhere at once. I'm sure I look like a deer caught in headlights in the pictures they're snapping. Thousands of them, if the never-ending shutter clicks are any indication.

They shout questions at me in rapid fire, so quick and loud that one is indecipherable from another. Nancy is standing by my side, and my arm is looped through hers for support. A large security guard named Dusty pushes his way through the crowd, clearing a path for us to follow.

Nancy warned me not to engage the vultures. "Keep your mouth shut and follow Dusty. Stare at his ass if you have to, but don't say a goddamn word," she said, before we left the building. Not a problem. I absolutely do not want to talk to these people.

The walk to the car seems never-ending, and even though I do my best to drown out the questions, a few of them make it through.

"Marisa, did you help your parents funnel money into offshore accounts?"

"Marisa, how do you feel about the downfall of the Blake empire?"

"Marisa, do you have any comment on yesterday's Post article about you and your sister enabling your parents' embezzlement?"

The word sister stops me in my tracks, and I send a death glare out into the crowd. I despise these people, picking at what's left of my family. I hate them almost as much as I hate my parents for what they've done, which is a lot. I don't know who asked the question, and I don't care. They all need to know that Corinne is off limits. They can ask me whatever questions they want, they can sling their allegations in my direction.

They can't touch *her*.

"My sister had nothing to do with this," I reply angrily. "And if any of you so much as suggest-"

Nancy yanks on my arm. When I look over at her, she's stone-faced, and tight-lipped. She glares at me, nodding at the car, indicating that we should keep on walking.

I know my outburst wasn't smart. If I had the chance to think it through, obviously I would've kept my mouth shut. But Corinne—my baby sister—absolutely cannot be touched by this scandal even more than she already has. I don't have control over much of anything these days, but I do have control over that. I won't allow it.

If that gets me in trouble with Nancy, so be it.

Dusty opens the car door, and Nancy gives me a subtle but firm push, letting me know that she's pissed. Once we're safely inside the car, the reporters' voices are muffled through the windows, and the full weight of what I just did sinks in.

"Do you understand that you just implicated yourself?"

Nancy pulls out her phone and starts typing. Her long, polished thumbnails click against the screen.

I do understand that. "Corinne stays out of it," I tell her. "No matter what."

"Honey, you don't get a say in what they print about you at this point. The best you can do is not give them any ammo, and you just gave them a ton of ammo. You hired me to make sure your business interests stay out of this mess, Marisa. Don't make that mess bigger than it already is."

I take a deep breath, and close my eyes on the exhale. I know she's right, I know I need to get a handle on my emotions. Much as I love Corrine and want to protect her, I'm not going to be any good for her now if I'm an unstable ball of anger. Even though I do my best to fight them, I feel the prickle of tears behind my eyes.

"Hey." Nancy takes my hand, and she angles her body toward mine in this cramped backseat. Her eyes are full of sympathy, and at this point she seems more like my therapist than my legal counsel. "I know this is difficult, Marisa. You just found out that most of what you've known your whole life is a lie."

That's putting it lightly.

I just found out that my parents are criminals. Liars. Cheats. I just found out that their businesses were built on cooked books, and that they've been stealing money from almost every client they had, for almost as long as they had them.

"Get a handle on this anger, sweetie. If you don't, you're going to make things worse. Trust me when I tell you that you don't want to do that."

"I won't blow up like that again," I assure her.

She gives my hand a squeeze before she turns away, and I huddle up against the door, resting my chin on my hand as I look out the window, wishing I was anywhere but here.

CHAPTER
Three

"What do you have on your face?" Corrine is laughing at me through my computer screen. It's the first video chat that we've had since she started her final semester in college, and I've missed her smiling face more than I can possibly express.

"It's seaweed, do you like it?" I turn my head to the left and the right, hollowing out my cheeks and giving her the best duck lips I'm capable of making.

"Very becoming. Is that for wrinkles or something?"

I do my best to look offended, but the dried gunk all over my skin makes that a little difficult. When I furrow my brow, a little bit of green seaweed dust sprinkles down onto my fluffy white cotton bathrobe.

"Hey, I'm only twenty seven! It's to prevent wrinkles, smartass. And don't be sarcastic about it, because one day you'll want to do this, too."

"You should go for a walk in Central Park with it on," she laughs.

I shake my head. "No one would bat an eye, Corinne. We've seen weirder things there than a lady in a seaweed mask. Hell, I've seen weirder on my way to the corner market."

"This is true." She sighs. "I really miss New York."

"You could always come back home." I'm not trying to send her on a guilt trip, but I wouldn't mind having her closer. She knows this, it's not new information.

Corinne furrows her brow. "I like California. Sun, almost perpetual summertime, fresh produce all-year long. No way."

"Can't blame me for trying. School's going well?"

"So far, yeah. My professors are all pretty great. I didn't read a single syllabus that struck fear into my heart like last semester." Corinne looks down at something, and I can hear the rustle of her sheets.

Unfortunately for her, I'm aware of all her little tics, and pulling on the corner of her sheets is one of them. She's got something on her mind. I'm not sure whether I should ask her, or give her the time and space to bring it up on her own. Ever since Mom and Dad got arrested, I've been worried about Corinne. She's completely resilient, but I want to ease the burden of this in whatever way that I can. I just can't do that unless she tells me what the burden is.

"I read about what you did yesterday," she tells me. She's still fumbling with the sheets, refusing to meet my eyes even though we're thousands of miles away from each other. "What you said in front of the reporters."

I square my shoulders, and sit up straight. I'm not sure why her comment puts me on edge, but it does. I feel like I have to be ready to defend myself. "I'm not going to let them bring your name into this, Corinne. They don't get to talk about you, and insinuate that you had anything to do with Mom and Dad's lies. Besides, I got a talking to from Nancy about it, anyway."

Corinne grins. "Good. I don't want you being stupid on my account."

"Who else would I be stupid for?" I frame it like a question, but really, she's the only person in my life that I'd put myself on the line for the way that I have.

She sighs, and rolls her eyes. When she finally looks at me, I can see that she's touched, but also a little annoyed.

"You know what I mean, Marisa. Your career is going well, the brand is taking off. I see people tweeting about it all the time. Don't do anything that messes that up, okay?"

Ah, the brand. The website, the lifestyle products... everything I worked so hard for and was proud to put my name on. Everything that my father deemed frivolous and wasteful and embarrassing to our family name. The brand that I hired Nancy to ensure was completely untouched by this goddamned scandal. I've never been so glad that in a moment of youthful, spiteful independence, I went out and got a loan for the startup cash, refusing to touch my trust fund or my savings. It was built on money that hadn't ever been touched by either one of my parents. We had fought about that, but it ended up being the best decision I've ever made, in retrospect.

And Corrine wants to make sure that I don't do anything stupid to jeopardize it.

"I just want you to have a normal life, Cor. I don't want your name in the newspapers, and I don't want anyone alleging you did anything as stupid and wrong as Mom and Dad did."

"I'm fine," she assures me. "It's just a few photographers and some reporters yelling things at me on campus sometimes. It's nothing that I can't handle. Besides, the bodyguard you hired that you think I don't know about keeps most of the trouble at bay."

I take a deep breath, and give her what is probably an incredibly sheepish, guilty look. The girl is so smart, I should've known that she'd figure it out sooner rather than later. What she doesn't know is that there's more than one person. I have a whole team looking after her.

"I'm not going to apologize for doing that, if that's what you're wanting from me."

Corinne smiles. "Not looking for an apology at all. I just wanted to let you know that I know that you did it."

"Good." In the moment that follows, I bite my lip and make a decision. "So, are you going to tell me what's bothering you?"

"You know. Of *course* you know."

And…she's messing with her sheets again.

"Of course I do," I reply. "So. Spill."

"It's silly." Corinne shakes her head, and pushes a fall of her curly blonde hair over her shoulder.

"If it's bothering you, it's not silly."

She sighs, and leans forward. "Do you remember my eleventh birthday party? The one where mom and dad basically rented out that water park?"

I was sixteen, and thought I was entirely too cool for a kid's birthday celebration. Corinne had begged me to get on a waterslide with her, and giving in to her resulted in one of my favorite pictures of the two of us. I have it just across my bedroom, framed on top of my dresser: me wrapped around Corrine, the two of us soaking wet and screaming as we dart out of the bottom of the slide, and into a giant wading pool.

"I remember," I say, although I can't quite figure out what's got her thinking about that day nearly ten years ago now. "What about it?"

She shrugs. "I can't stop wondering if someone else's kid didn't get to have a day like that because of what Mom and Dad did."

Oh. Corinne's kind heart and thoughtful soul still manage to catch me off guard sometimes. I take a moment to think about the right answer to her question; one that will be honest but still put her at ease.

"Cor, Mom and Dad stole money from incredibly rich

people over a long period of time. They skimmed off the top for decades, so that no one would figure out what they were doing. Mom and Dad did a shitty thing, but I don't think anyone went without because of it." If there's any silver lining in this situation, it's that our parents didn't bilk poor people out of their hard-earned money, although at this point I wouldn't put it past them. I think my mother and father are capable of things that Corinne and I could never dream of. These past couple of months have proven that.

Corrine gives me this skeptical look, like she really wants to believe me, but she can't quite let herself do it.

"They did have their own money," I remind her. "You know Gran and Pop were rich." Mom and Dad just squandered that money away on bad investment after bad investment and who knows what else. Then they took to stealing to make up for it.

She nods. "Okay."

I'm relieved that she doesn't need any more assurances.

"I'm going to pay you back for my tuition."

"What? No you're not." I paid her most recent tuition bill, because she's not going to attend college paid for with stolen money.

"Marisa-"

"No. You're going to study hard, and you're going to graduate. You're going to do great things, and make people forget that our parents are shitty, lying thieves."

"Okay." She reluctantly smiles. "I think I can accept those

terms."

It's not like she has any choice in the matter. "Good."

"And how are things for you?"

I shrug. "Can't complain."

Corinne raises her brow, and I know that she doesn't believe me, but she isn't going to call me out on it. I like playing the protector where she's concerned, and she's very gracious about humoring me with that.

"The Murphy Building thing is this weekend, isn't it?"

"Yeah." I nod. I've been working on putting this benefit together for months now. Now that my name is in the press for something my parents did, a few of the ladies who lunch want to kick me off the board and take my name off of anything pertaining to the benefit.

I care about the building and its restoration too much let them get away with that.

"I take it they weren't successful in removing you?"

"No," I reply with a smirk. "They were not."

There isn't a chance in hell that I'm going to let them erase me from this, not when it was my idea. Not when I did the hard work to make it happen. I'm going to walk into that benefit with my head held high.

Corinne smirks at me, reminding me of the young woman that she was before this whole scandal came to light. Defiant, smart, and carefree. It's a smirk that makes me glad I stood up to these women. It makes me want to make Corinne proud.

"Give 'em hell. And report back to me after."

That's exactly what I'm gonna do.

CHAPTER
four

"This turnout is pathetic," Mitzi Vandergraff says, as she surveys said pathetic crowd. She's the only person I know who manages to look simultaneously elegant and, well…like a complete bitch. Her arms are crossed over the (probably) hand-beaded bodice of her couture gown, as she rolls her eyes. "I was right to want you off the board, Marisa. *They* wanted to keep you to spare your feelings." She sweeps her perfectly manicured hand toward the other architectural board members standing to our right, who look just as worried about the turnout as I feel. "But I told them it was a terrible idea."

"Luckily you never worry about sparing anyone's feelings," I reply dryly. The sentiment isn't as cutting as it could be considering she's absolutely right.

I told Corinne that I was going to come in here and give

'em hell, but all the fight is draining from me. The me-against-the-world attitude that's been keeping me going lately has all but fizzled out. For the first time since my parents' scandal broke, I feel defeated.

Not wanting to stand in Mitzi's judgmental presence for a second longer than I have to, I excuse myself to mingle. I walk through the crowd, looking for a friendly face, for an opening to a conversation. Anything.

I'm hit hard by this low attendance. Usually at events like this, the din of the crowd drowns out the ambient music, but the six-piece orchestra is loud and clear tonight.

This fundraiser is a dud, as much as it pains me to admit it. What hurts even more is that it's all my fault.

Why didn't I just step down? Being a Blake is social poison right now, and if it wasn't for my pride…

"Marisa?" asks a familiar voice, as the hand belonging to the owner of that voice rests on my forearm.

I turn and see Caleb Simmons. He's one of Ben's best friends, and someone that I considered to be a good friend of mine, too, once upon a time. We only ever talk to each other once in a while. Not very often at all since Ben and I broke up.

That's one of the things that makes breakups even worse, I think. The divvying up of possessions and friendships. When Ben and I were together, Caleb and I were pretty close. After the breakup, we're really nothing more than cordial acquaintances.

I knew I could count on him to show up tonight, despite the scandal attached to my rapidly devaluing last name. He's just that kind of guy.

"Hi!" If I'm a little over-enthusiastic, can you blame me? His is the first friendly face I've seen all night.

Caleb gives me a warm smile, one that I remember him wearing so often when we first met. He opens his arms to me and I go in for a hug.

"How are *you*?" I ask, my voice muffled against his shoulder.

"I'm doing well," he replies. I can tell that his answer is sincere, and he's not just putting me on, like some people who run in our circle have a tendency to do. Hesitantly he asks, "And you?"

I offer him a half-hearted smile and a shrug. "Been better, but you probably know that. Tonight certainly isn't helping." I gesture to the room around me, still looking about as pathetic as Mitzi said it was, all things considered.

"You know what? Fuck 'em." Caleb tips back a sip of champagne, and I can't help but laugh. It's a shame that everything that happened between Ben and me strained things between me and Caleb, because I've missed him. He always did know how to make me look on the bright side of things, even where his best friend's shitty behavior was concerned.

"Hey," I say, leaning in close so that no one will overhear me. "My parents didn't…you know?" I can't bring myself to outright ask him if my parents stole from him, although I have to know.

"No." His brows furrow together as he considers his words. "Your father contacted my secretary a few times, but—no offense—I never took any of his meetings."

A wave of relief washes over me, and I let out a long exhale. "Thank god. No offense taken. That's probably shaping up to be one of your better business decisions, don't you think?"

"Marisa…"

He has this look on his face that most people get when I try to make light of the situation, but it's the only way I know how to deal with this. "It's okay. I know joking about it makes it awkward, but I'm not really sure how to deal with it otherwise."

Caleb nods; I know he understands. There was a time when he knew me well enough to understand my coping mechanisms, and it looks like that knowledge has carried over through the years. He knows exactly where I'm coming from.

"So, what have you been up to? Ben filled me in on the mini empire you're building," he says casually. "He said you have a new site up and running. I checked it out earlier. The functionality is amazing. My girlfriend loves it."

I'm sure my mouth is hanging open, because he just casually dropped a Ben bomb and then moved right along with the conversation. I'm having trouble processing the information. Ben is aware of what I've been doing with my business? He knows about my site?

"Ben…" I can't quite figure out what I want to say next, or which question out of the thousands that are floating through my mind I should ask first. I settle on, "What?"

"Caleb!" Mitzi sidles up right in between us.

Caleb schools the exasperated irritation that flashes across his face in a second. "It's so good to see you! I'm glad you decided to come despite the…" she shoots me a dirty look, her perfectly lined beady little eyes narrowed into tiny slits. "Circumstances."

With a tight smile, Caleb says, "It's a pleasure to come out and support a cause that my friend is so passionate about."

Mitzi preens under Caleb's compliment, and the sight of it turns my stomach.

"And," Caleb continues as he steps to the side, "I was in the middle of talking to that friend, so if you'll excuse me."

If I could bottle up the look of undignified horror on Mitzi's face as she realizes that Caleb has just dismissed her, I'm pretty sure I could live off of it for a year.

She walks off, scandalized, and I just want to hug Caleb again.

"Thank you," I say gratefully, as I grab a flute of champagne off of the tray of a waiter passing by.

"My pleasure." He grins in that playful way I remember, whenever he, Ben, and their other friend Oliver were up to something. "I know she was pushing to have you removed from the committee."

I furrow my brow. "How did you know that?"

"Ben filled Oliver in on it, and they, in turn, told me. Oh." He pats at his breast pocket. "Oliver couldn't come, but he sent me with a check."

I smile. "Thank you. And I'll be sure to thank him, too. But…Ben. How did Ben know about the committee? How did Ben know about my site, and-"

"Hey." A pretty brunette in a stunningly gorgeous dress slings her arm around Caleb's, and he beams down at her like she's the sun.

"Hey there." He gives her a kiss, followed by this dopey little grin. It's such a far cry from the detached, closed-off guy that I knew in college that the whole exchange takes me back a bit. Still, I can't help but smile at them. They're one of those disgusting couples who just radiate bliss.

Apparently they're also one of those couples who forget about the world around them when they're around each other, because it takes Caleb about a full minute to remember that there are other people in the room.

He shakes his head, remembering himself.

"Marisa, this is Mia, my girlfriend. Mia," he says purposefully, giving a pointed nod in my direction, "this is Marisa."

Mia's whole face lights up at the mention of my name; she reaches out and enthusiastically shakes my hand. "It's so nice to meet you," she says. "I've heard so much about you."

Caleb clears his throat, and if I didn't know better, I'd swear he was warning her to be quiet, probably to keep her from telling me everything that she's heard about me. Which…why is she hearing things about me, exactly? I feel like I'm in some kind of twilight zone.

Ben—ex-boyfriend Ben, serial cheater and breaker of my heart Ben—is reading up on me? He's following my life and my work and telling his friends about it?

Mia must get a sense that I'm about to barrage her with questions. "Caleb told me a lot about you," she hedges, even though I know it's a lie. She's so sweet I don't call her out on it. "You two knew each other in college?"

I nod, then take a sip of my champagne. "We did, and I somehow lived to tell the tale."

Mia and Caleb let out a chuckle, then Mia looks a bit wistful. "I would've liked to have known Caleb back then."

"I don't know if this will disappoint you or make you happy, but I don't have any scandalous stories about him. Caleb was always the perfect gentleman when I was around."

Mia narrows her eyes at me like she doesn't believe me, but I'm telling her the truth. Caleb treated me better than Ben ever did, often times sticking around in the aftermath of a breakup, offering me a pint of mint chip and a shoulder to cry on.

"Did Caleb tell you that Oliver couldn't make it tonight?" Mia asks.

I nod.

Caleb laughs. "I told you I wasn't going to forget."

Mia shrugs. "I just wanted to make sure. Ben should be here any second," she says, scanning the crowd. "I told him not to be late, but he's late."

I invited him, so the fact that he's coming isn't a complete surprise, but knowing that his appearance is imminent makes my heart skip a beat.

I'm not sure I want to examine the reason for that too closely.

"Marisa," Caleb starts, and I know for sure that I don't want to hear what he's going to say. I have a feeling that it's going to be exactly what I don't want to hear: that Ben's changed, that he really means it this time, that he wants to give us another shot. "Look, about Ben…"

I just…I can't hear that right now.

"I'm sorry, I just remembered that I have a…I have a thing I have to attend to over there." I hope I sound as friendly as I'm trying to sound, and not completely like I'm bailing, even though Caleb knows me well enough to know that I'm bailing. "I'll see you two before you leave?"

Mia gives me a friendly smile. "Maybe we can meet up for coffee sometime?"

I nod. Yes, coffee. "Sure, that sounds wonderful."

I practically trip over my own feet as I make my way to the door, desperate for some fresh air.

CHAPTER
Five

The Murphy Building is an exquisite structure in a city full of exquisite structures. Sure, its cracked marble stairway needs some repairs, and the grand, ornate columns along the front that stretch up toward the sky aren't as polished and unblemished as they used to be. In a place like New York—where every inch of real estate is precious—the fact that such a beautiful building fell into this state of disrepair is appalling.

It's always been one of my favorite places in the city, ever since I was old enough to climb to the top of the stairs on my own. I'd look out at the crowded streets full of taxis and buses, the sidewalks packed with people hurrying from here to there. For the first time in my young life, in a city that is so easy to get lost in, I felt big.

My nanny would take me on picnics here on my first and last days of school. She'd lift me up onto the short marble ledge that ran along the East side of the building, then pull herself up to sit beside me. We'd eat peanut butter and jelly sandwiches with the crusts cut off, and dangle our legs while we ate, our heels clicking against the concrete wall.

Ben kissed me for the first time on the steps of this building. I was a freshman in college, and he was a sophomore. We met in the library at Columbia, when Ben bumped into me in the stacks. I had my arms full of books, and he helped me carry them to my table. He took a seat next to me, and walked me through Professor Calderon's syllabus. He had taken a class with her the year before, and was familiar with the assignments.

He sat a little too close, his shoulder brushing mine. We leaned over the paper together, smiling at each other as I made notes in the margins. He smelled like soap and spice, and I wanted to know what his full, pink lips tasted like.

Later that afternoon, we went on a New York native's tour of our favorite places. He walked me across Bow Bridge, and I brought him here, to this building. There was a street performer playing the violin, and Ben danced me across the promenade. We both laughed when he dipped me, and after, he brushed the backs of his fingers across my blushing cheek. I was breathless from wanting him so badly, and when his lips touched mine, I knew my life wouldn't ever be the same again.

If I knew then about the heartbreak and the pain that would follow that perfect kiss, I wonder…would I have done anything differently?

"Hey." Ben's voice pulls me out of my thoughts.

I wish I could say that I'm surprised to see him standing here, but that sixth sense of his must be in full effect tonight. I'm definitely feeling emotionally vulnerable, so of course he found me.

"Hey," I reply, trying really hard not to notice how good he looks in his suit. It's completely unfair, really. He looks like he's just stepped out of a magazine, or he's fresh off of a runway, or like he's getting ready to go deep undercover in some ridiculous spy movie. The most unfair part of it is that I know he looks this good with absolutely no prep time whatsoever. He probably just stepped out of the shower, towel dried his hair, and got dressed.

I know that routine from experience, because I've seen it before with my own eyes. The reminder of that intimacy we used to share tugs at my heart, and I do my best to tamp it down. Feeling all fuzzy and reminiscent about Ben is what gets me into trouble, every damn time.

"You look beautiful." His voice is soft, and there's the hint of a smile on his lips.

"Thank you," I reply. I think about telling him that he looks good, too, but I'm not sure if I should. That might take the conversation in a direction I'm incredibly unprepared for.

"May I?" Ben motions to the empty space beside me on the bench.

I move to the right, making a little more room for him. "Sure."

As Ben sits down, my gaze wanders over to the empty arrival lane in front of the building. There aren't any cars there. Everyone who's going to show up to this benefit is already inside, and that was a pretty low number. I feel a depressing little wave roll inside of my stomach.

"You're late," I tell him.

He looks down at his hands. "I know. I'm sorry, I got held up in a meeting that I couldn't get out of. I wanted to be here when-" He stops himself from saying whatever it was that was going to come out of his mouth next.

"When what?" My curiosity is always going to get the better of me when it comes to this man.

He shrugs. "I didn't want you to be here on your own. Not that you would've been, I mean, I just know that…"

"Caleb told me that you were pretty well-versed on my situation with the architectural board." I'm aiming for light and breezy, because I don't want to reprimand him, but seriously… why does he know so much about what's been going on with me lately?

"My mother brought it up over brunch not too long ago."

Okay, so his mother fed him the information; he wasn't driven by his own curiosity to go out looking for it. The realization makes me feel…well, I'm not sure how I feel about it. I don't like that the first emotion I felt was disappointment, that's for sure.

"Mia will be glad you're here," I say, twisting my fingers together on my lap.

Ben grins. "You met her?"

"She and Caleb are inside, forgetting that there are other people in the room," I tease.

"Yeah, they tend to do that." Ben huffs out a laugh.

"They seem really happy."

"Disgustingly so, which is probably the best kind of happy to be."

It's odd, hearing Ben talk like this. Being wistful about relationships really isn't his thing. It didn't used to be, at least. His elbows are resting on his knees. He keeps rubbing his palms together, and looking down at them as if they hold the answer to some kind of question that he hasn't asked aloud.

"Probably. It was nice of him to come," I say, trying to fill up the silence that feels like it's stretching into forever.

"But you're surprised to see me." Ben looks at me, understanding written all over his face.

No point in lying now.

"I am." This isn't the first time we've both been invited to the same function, but it is the first time I've seen him at one since we broke up. I know that's not a coincidence. "Showing up at my house the other day, talking to Oliver and Caleb about me, being here…why now?"

He shrugs, and looks down at his hands again. If I didn't

know any better, I'd think that he was nervous. But Ben Williams has never been nervous around me, unless he was worried that he was about to get caught in some kind of a lie.

"I've missed you, Marisa. I asked Caleb to come here tonight, because I was worried that it might be difficult, seeing you."

"You just saw me," I say with a short laugh. "A lot of me."

I'm desperate to lighten up this conversation. I need something to loosen up this knot of longing that's coiling up in my stomach, making me want him again. It won't end well, I tell myself for the thousandth time. It never ends well for me when Ben is concerned.

"I asked him to come here before I went to see you the other night. Do…" He rubs the back of his neck. "Do we need to talk about that? About what happened?"

"No," I reply, my eyebrows scrunching together. "Why would we need to talk about it? It was just sex, Ben. That seems to be what most of our relationship was built on." I'm not even bitter about it at this point, it's just a simple statement of fact, one that took me years to come to grips with.

"Marisa." Ben has a way of saying my name that sends a shiver down my spine, electrifying every nerve ending down to my toes. This time is no different. His voice is deep and serious, and my eyes are immediately drawn to his. "You were never just sex to me."

I roll my eyes, because that is such a typical, smooth, old-school Ben thing to say, and it helps me remember to keep my wits about me when things between us start to get hot and heavy. Because they will again, I know. I'd be foolish to pretend otherwise.

Ben must get the hint that I don't want to delve any further into that particular conversation, because he asks, "Why are you out here?"

"Mitzi Vandergraff," I say. "She was reminding me of my failures earlier, and…well, there's a lot going on in there tonight, and not much of it is good. I thought that getting some air would help me…" I motion to my head, "get control of what's going on in here."

"What did Mitzi do this time?"

"She reminded me that she wanted me off of the architectural board, and that she was right to want it, judging by the turn out tonight. And is she wrong?" I ask, feeling like I'm just teetering on the edge of being hysterical, even though I'm trying so hard to put a lid on that. "This thing with my parents is tainting the fundraising. Who wants to rub elbows with the daughter of people who stole from them?"

"Anyone with half a brain knows that you didn't have anything to do with that, no matter what the tabloids say. And Mitzi doesn't fall into the category of people with half a brain."

I want to smile, but I just can't. I shake my head, then fold my arms across my chest. "I really want to fix this building, and I let my pride get in the way."

"A lot of good things happened here," he says, and I wonder if Ben actually remembers what some of those things were, if he remembers our first date. I wonder if he remembers all the times we came here together after. "I can't imagine anyone more capable of fixing this place."

They're the words I needed to hear at the moment I needed to hear them. I'm going to blame that rush of emotion on what I do next.

I lean in, and press my lips against his. I grip his lapels and pull him close. This isn't smart. It isn't smart, but *I don't care.*

I whisper, "Make me forget about everything that's happened. Just…tonight, please. Make me forget."

"When did you get this scar?" Ben asks, sliding his rough hand along my shoulder. In the post-orgasmic bliss that followed round one, I didn't kick him out of my bed, a decision that I'm sure I'm going to regret sooner rather than later.

"When I was seven," I reply, nuzzling my head into my pillow. I don't really feel like having some personal, deep, explore-our-scars together conversation, but this is literally a superficial question, and I don't want Ben to go just yet. It's still kind of early, and I'm counting on at least another couple of orgasms before I set him free. "My mom had this Shih-Tzu that I'm positive came straight from Hell. It hated me. I was lying on the floor one day reading a book, and it attacked me for absolutely no reason. I had to get stitches and everything. The rabies shot really scandalized my mother."

Ben lets out this low, breathy chuckle. The pad of his thumb skims the raised flesh of my scar, and the bed shifts as he leans forward and presses a kiss to it. I can't help the physical reaction that his tenderness teases out of me, and goosebumps break out across my skin. If he feels me shiver after, thankfully he doesn't say anything about it.

"I never noticed it before," he replies quietly.

I open my mouth, a cutting remark finding its way right to the edge of my tongue. I clamp my lips together before I let it out, though. After we just had pretty amazing sex, when I'm comfortable, and Ben is running a soothing hand up and down my skin, it doesn't feel right to take a dig at him.

This, he notices. And he speaks up. "You can say it."

"I wasn't going to say anything," I lie.

"Yes you were." The words are soft, and not accusatory at all. "You can say it."

"I was just..." Even with permission, giving voice to my thoughts doesn't feel right at all, but I know that Ben isn't going to drop it until I confess. "I've had that scar for years. You've seen me naked how many times, and you never noticed it before?"

His hand stills. "I didn't notice a lot of things about you when I had the chance."

I hate the way the tenderness in his voice tricks me into

CASSIE CROSS

thinking that he means what he's saying. How many times have I heard a line like this from him? How many times has he held me in his arms, told me how much he regretted the way he treated me, and promised to do better in the future? He knows these are words that get to me, that saying them like this will make me weak. The making up, the convincing, those are the parts of this that he's so good at, and they're the reasons I need to watch myself whenever I'm with him. It's so easy to believe what he says, to believe that he wants this and that we can make it work this time.

God, I want to believe him. It would be so easy to let his words wrap around me, and to lose myself in this thing between us. I've been burned by him too many times, though, and I'm not sure I could come back from it another time.

"Ben," I whisper. "Please don't."

He gives my shoulder a gentle tug. I don't fight it, and roll over until I'm facing him.

"Hey," he says, crooking his finger under my chin.

It takes a moment for me to bring my eyes up to meet his. If I could just do all of this without having to look at him, to see what I always want to believe is honesty in his eyes, then maybe keeping this strictly sex would be easier.

Ben leans forward, gently brushing his lips against mine. "I know I hurt you," be begins, tangling his fingers in my hair. "I know there's nothing I can do that will ever erase that. But I want to try and make up for it."

38

"You don't have to make up for it," I reply. There's a knot in my throat growing tighter by the second, and the more he talks, the more difficult it's going to be for me to keep the tears from falling. It was stupid of me to let him back into my life, back into my bed, but what's done is done.

"I do need to make up for it. I want to make up for it."

"Ben." I have no idea what I'm going to say next. What can I say? He's never said these exact words to me, but the sentiment is usually the same. He's sorry he hurt me, he won't do it again.

This time isn't any different. It's not *any different.*

"I'm so sorry. For everything. I loved you then, but I needed time to catch up with what I was feeling. I never stopped loving you, I still-"

I press my lips against his to get him to stop talking. I cannot hear the words he was getting ready to say; they would be the beginning of the end for me, and I'm barely hanging on as it is.

Instead, I kiss away his declaration with frantic, unbridled passion, our lips and tongues tangling together.

"Okay," he says, when he both pull away breathless. "Okay."

I get the sense that he's giving up today, but he's not giving up forever. I need to occupy his mind before anything else happens that we can't take back, so I slide down his body, watching goosebumps pucker all over his skin as I trail my fingernails along the hard lines of his abs. God, his body is perfect. Always has been - it's almost not fair.

I settle myself between his legs, then plant my hand on the mattress beside his hip, using the other one to stroke his already rock-hard length.

He thrusts up into my hand, lets out this strangled, sexy noise when I close my lips around the tip of his cock.

"Fuck," he says, easily distracted. He wraps his big hand around the back of my head, and I open my mouth to him, sliding my tongue along his length. "That's it," he says. "I love your mouth."

These are the only words I can handle from him right now.

CHAPTER
Six

"So," Corinne says, running her fingers through her hair. "How did the fundraiser go?"

We've been chatting for about fifteen minutes, mostly about Corrine's course load. She must have known that I didn't want to talk about it, given that she held out for so long to ask.

I take a deep breath, and purse my lips together, figuring out what exactly I want to tell her. That Mitzi Vandergraff is a bitch? That she was right? Do I tell her about Caleb and Ben, or do I just keep it simple? She's pretty good at reading me, so she'll know if I try to sell her a lie.

"It didn't go so well," I admit. "We didn't meet our goal. It was basically a public exercise in humiliation for me. And the board, I guess, since I was on it."

"Let me guess," Corrine says with a sigh. "Mitzi Vandergraff strikes again?"

I shrug, then run my fingertips along the edge of the quilt on my bed. "She wasn't wrong this time, though. I should've removed myself from the board like she wanted. Fighting my removal was selfish, Cor. If I really wanted to get the money for the restoration, I wouldn't have fought them just out of spite."

"You didn't stay on out of spite," Corrine says with a gentle smile. "You love that building; you're more qualified to fight for money to restore it than anyone else on that board is."

"That's exactly why I should've stepped down." Since I left the benefit early, hoping that the absence of my presence would compel people to donate if they wouldn't have otherwise, Mitzi had to call me to give me an update on how much money we raised. Her slightly gleeful tone as she let me know that we missed the mark has been haunting me ever since I heard it that day.

"Well, what's done is done." Corinne's voice is resigned, like she's realized that it's pointless to even try to convince me that I should've done anything other than what I did. "You would've felt guilty if you stepped down, I know you. You did what you thought was right, and that's one of the things that I love most about you, Marisa. You don't let people intimidate you."

"I didn't used to let people intimidate me," I correct.

Corinne rolls her eyes at me. Years of being on the receiving end of that look makes me sure that she's being playful. "You still don't. Come on, that hasn't changed. You just had a bad night between what happened with Mom and Dad, and people acting like assholes. The fact that you care so much and things didn't work out the way you hoped they would makes it worse. You weren't alone all night, were you?"

I shake my head. I know she has this vision of me standing in the corner by myself, watching everyone interact, the odd woman out.

"No," I reply. "Caleb was there. He brought along his new girlfriend."

"She's cute," Corinne says. "I saw some pictures of her."

"She really is cute. And incredibly nice. And you can tell that Caleb really loves her. It was actually a little bit gross being around them."

"Never thought I'd see the day."

I laugh. "Me neither."

She leans back against her headboard, and I see her fiddling with her sheet like she always does when she's hesitant to ask me something.

"Just ask," I say, trying not to sound as annoyed as I feel. I know what the question is going to be.

"Felicity told me that Ben was planning on going." She cringes when she finishes asking, like she's waiting for me to be offended or angry that she's been talking about Ben and me with his sister. I'm feeling a twinge of regret about introducing them back when Ben and I were still together, if they're going to start conspiring against me and getting involved in my love life. Not that I have a love life with Ben anymore.

"Felicity has a big mouth," I tease, because I'm not quite sure how to answer a question that she hasn't asked me yet. "I should fire her."

"You're not her boss."

This is true. "Well, I could not hire her again," I say with a smile.

"Oh, please. That spread you brought her on to style got the most hits on your site."

"Shh." I smile at her, because I love her so much. "You shouldn't hang out with her. She's a bad influence."

Corinne grins. "Terrible news, then. She's in town for a shoot, and we're meeting up for dinner tomorrow night."

Oh god, I'm sure they're going to start plotting and planning something, like some weird alternate reality version of *The Parent Trap*.

"Remember to mind your own business," I warn. "And make sure she buys you dinner."

"Marisa," Corinne whines. "You aren't going to answer me?"

I bite my lip, then decide, what the hell? "Yes, he was there. And that's all I'm going to tell you about it."

CHAPTER
Seven

I sit alone at a table in the middle of an incredibly upscale restaurant, which is filled with the type of people that I spend a lot of time trying to avoid. The only reason I'm here is because Mitzi Vandergraff asked me to meet her here, and I was intrigued enough to say yes.

Mitzi, of course, is late. She still believes that we're living in a world where people regularly make fashionably late entrances.

The waitress brings me another glass of wine. I'm on my third already; hopefully Mitzi shows up before I'm completely plowed. Otherwise, I might say some things I'll wind up regretting, especially since I'm not really sure why she asked me to meet her here in the first place. I stepped down from the board for the Murphy Building restoration. What more does she want from me?

I showed up early, knowing that I needed a little bit of a buzz going if I was going to deal with her, but I don't want things to get out of hand. My reputation just can't take another hit right now.

The next time the waitress walks by, I order an appetizer. I've got to get a little food in me.

When Mitzi finally shows up, I'm drinking the very last drop of red out of my wine glass. She waltzes in like she owns the place, turning heads as she walks by. Even a casual bystander who didn't know her could tell she loves the attention. That she notices it, and craves it.

"Sorry I'm late," she says as the host pulls out her chair for her.

I know that she doesn't mean it.

"To what do I owe this honor? I already resigned from the board, so I'm not sure what business we have left." I ask. I think I do a pretty good job at not slurring my words.

"I didn't want to have to be the one to tell you this," she says, and my pulse automatically kicks into overdrive.

"Didn't want to have to tell me what?" Despite the buzz I have going on right now, I have no desire to sit here and let her drag things out, to torture me with some kind of soul-crushing cutdown.

She pulls her absurdly large handbag into her lap, and reaches inside. She pulls out a piece of paper, and slides it across the freshly pressed linen tablecloth. Her red-painted lips are pressed into a tight line, and she's drumming her fingernails (painted in a matching shade) on the tabletop. She declines when the waiter asks her for her order; she doesn't even ask for a glass of water.

It's so typically Mitzi to call me into a place like this for a hit-and-run.

I reach over and pull the paper toward me, bracing myself for whatever is written on there. I hesitate to open it, liking my life the way it is just fine without knowing whatever information is waiting for me inside. Is it some kind of bribe? Is it bad news? Is she going to blackmail me with something? I honestly don't know what to expect where she's concerned.

Cautiously, like it contains explosives, I unfold the paper. There's a long list, two columns wide. Names and dollar amounts. It's a list of donations, and I scan through it quickly. When my eyes meet the sum at the bottom of the page, I nearly cry.

"We met our goal?" I ask, with a completely undignified squeal, which makes some of the snooty clientele sitting around us stare. My heart is pounding with the thrill of victory, the first one I've felt since the news broke about my parents, and maybe even before that. "We met our goal." I repeat as I look at the total again, in shock. *No*, we *exceeded* our goal.

"Looks like we miscalculated and I gave you the wrong total. The people who attended decided to take pity on you with their checkbooks after all."

I'm so happy about this that I can't even drum up enough anger or annoyance to tell her to go to Hell. That's how excited I am. My foot is bouncing, the bottom of my heel tapping against the hardwood floor. Adrenaline makes my fingertips all tingly, and enhances the effect of all the wine I've drunk. This is great news, not only because I love the Murphy Building and I want to see it returned to its former glory, but also because *in your face, Mitzi Vandergraff.*

In. Your. Face.

"Congratulations," Mitzi says, and only she can make what should be a nice sentiment sound so bitchily terrible.

"I'm keeping this," I say, folding the paper up and putting it in my purse. My stomach rumbles, and I decide that I absolutely do not want to spend any more of my precious time sitting here with someone like Mitzi when I'm feeling so over the moon about my success. I'm in a good mood, a little bit tipsy, and I want to go have an actual lunch (not froufrou hors d'ouvres from this place) at my favorite restaurant near the Murphy Building. I want to feel the relief and excitement for what I had a hand in accomplishing.

I just can't believe that we exceeded our goal. It's more than I could've ever hoped for.

I say goodbye to Mitzi, walk outside, and hail a cab in front of the restaurant.

When we hit a patch of traffic, I pull the paper out of my purse, taking a look at who donated what. I'm going to send each and every one of them a hand-written thank you note. I'm already working up some of the messages in my head when my gaze falls on a particularly large donation. A donation that makes up almost a third of what we needed.

When I see the name, my heart stops.

Ben Williams.

CHAPTER

Eight

'm sitting at a corner table in my favorite restaurant, one that has just as many good memories as bad ones for me. The french onion soup that I order every time I come in here does a lot to erase those bad memories, though.

The list of donations is unfolded in front of me, and I stare at Ben's name in between bites of my soup. My eyes keep repeating a circuit between Ben's name and the amount he donated. The shock of it still hasn't worn off. I mean, Ben might not have been very generous with his heart when we were together, but I knew he was a generous man when it came to the way he spent his time and his money. I'm not surprised he donated; that building holds what I'm assuming are some good memories for him, too.

But that building is everything to me, and this isn't a donation so much as a saving grace.

What I'm having a difficult time figuring out is...why? The donation must have come in after the fundraiser, so did he do it because he knew we came up short of our goal? Is this some kind of grand gesture? Old Ben always did go for gestures of the sweeping romantic kind. He always figured that one big move was more important than the little things that meant more, at least to me.. Is this more of that? A romantic gesture to get my attention? He knows how desperate I was to fund this project. Did he do this for me? For a tax write-off? So I wouldn't cut off the sex?

I take another sip of my soup, when-

"Marisa?"

It's Ben, of course. I don't even need to look up from my bowl. His voice has always set every nerve in my body on edge, and it's no different now. Goosebumps break out all over my skin when I look up at his stupid, unfairly handsome face. Why does he have to look so *good* all the time?

I quickly pull the paper off the tabletop, try (and fail) to discreetly slide it back into the outside pocket of my purse. Ben follows my movement with his eyes, but he turns away just as soon as I catch him.

"Hey," I reply with a smile.

"How are you? Everything okay?"

I take a deep breath and nod. "Yes, absolutely. How are you?"

He shrugs and shoves his hands into the pockets of his

ridiculously well-cut suit.

"I can't complain. I had a meeting nearby that got canceled. Thought I'd stop by for some lunch."

I nod absently, looking down at my bowl of soup. "I hope you enjoy."

When I look up, he gives me a tight smile. If I didn't know him as well as I do, I would've missed the flash of disappointment in his eyes.

"Thanks," he says wistfully. "You too."

It's not until he turns away from me that I realize that I don't want him to go. After saving my ass with the Murphy Building benefit, and actually caring enough to help us meet our goal, the very least I can do is invite him to sit down and have lunch with me.

"Ben?"

He turns. "Yeah?" The disappointment I saw earlier has been replaced with an earnest hopefulness that was always the end of my willpower where this man was concerned.

"Have lunch with me," I say, motioning to the chair across from me. "If you want to. Please."

His eyebrows raise in surprise, and it's actually kind of cute. "Really?"

I can't help but let out a short laugh. "Yes, really."

"I'd love to." He doesn't even finish his reply before he pulls out the chair, and unbuttons his blazer as he takes a seat.

When the waiter comes back around a minute or so later, I

ask him for another menu, and request that he holds my order until Ben's is ready.

After he takes a sip of water, Ben says, "You're in a much better mood than you were the last time I saw you."

I know I promised myself I'd keep things light with him, and that includes steering clear of these emotional minefields that the two of us always seem to have difficulty navigating, but I can't help myself today. Not after learning about what he did.

"I am in a good mood," I admit.

"I'm glad," he replies. "It suits you."

"Thank you." I do my best to fight the blush that I can feel rushing to my cheeks.

"Is it okay if I ask what got you in this mood?"

I know he's doing a little digging here, hoping he'll get a personal piece of information along with my actual answer.

"I just had a meeting with Mitzi Vandergraff."

He looks puzzled. "I don't think I've ever met a person who was even remotely happy after spending time with that woman."

I let out a loud, unexpected laugh.

Ben's eyes widen, but he laughs along with me, even though he's obviously confused by my outburst.

"I haven't heard you laugh in a long time," he says with a gentle smile.

There's a good reason for that; I haven't felt like laughing around him in years. But now is not the time for such admissions. That would only hurt him, and hurting him is the very last thing I want to do right now.

"It's nice," Ben adds, before I have a chance to reply.

"It's because of you."

His eyes are even wider than they were just a second before. "What? Why?"

Cat's out of the bag at this point, no use in trying to walk around it. I reach down into my purse, pull out the piece of paper I was looking at right before he showed up, and slide it across the table.

"Ben." His name comes out much more tenderly than I meant it to.

When he realizes what I'm showing him, he breathes a soft, "Oh."

"Why did you do this?" I'm careful to keep my voice soft, because I don't want him to think that I'm accusing him of anything. I really just want to know why, what the angle is, if there is one. "Was it some kind of grand gesture, or were you trying to-"

"No," he says vehemently. "It wasn't a grand gesture. Well, it was a gesture, just not a grand one. I know how much that building means to you, Marisa. I would've done this regardless of whether you ever spoke to me again or not. Sorry I was late with it." He clears his throat, and reaches up to adjust his tie. "I was...distracted before I got to go inside."

I can't help but smile at the way he explains his tardiness, but I'm still curious. "Why, then?"

He shrugs. "We went on our first date there. We made memories there. That place is special to me too, Marisa. I don't like seeing it falling apart."

Not really sure how to respond to that, I fiddle with the napkin that's splayed out across my lap. "I didn't think…"

"You didn't think what?"

"I didn't know that place meant anything to you. That those memories were special for you."

Ben looks down, and turns his glass of water between his index finger and thumb. "Yeah, I…I can see why you might believe that."

Even though I know I shouldn't ask this, I do it anyway. "Why is it different now?"

I wasn't ready to hear the answer to this question the other day, but all the fear that I've been feeling about finding out what Ben is playing at has morphed into an irritating curiosity. I have to know what's going on, what the end game is here.

"Why is what different now?"

"Why are those memories special to you now? Why is the Murphy Building special to you now?" What I leave unspoken is the question that I want to ask the most: why am *I* special to him now? Instead, I say, "None of it seemed to matter to you much when it should have."

He looks down, and takes a deep breath. "I deserve that."

Yes, he does.

"I was trying to tell you before, Marisa. I needed my head to catch up with my heart. I was stupid back then. I wasn't ready for you when I had you, and it's one of the biggest regrets of my life."

They're the words that younger me always longed to hear, and they're the words that older me just cannot afford to believe. Believing them means that I'm ready to risk my heart with this man again, and I cannot. Still, the sick, sadistic part of me has to ask.

"And you are now? Ready for me, I mean."

He swallows so hard that I can actually see it. "Yes." His voice is rough, and god help me...he looks sincere. "But I know you aren't ready to believe me."

He's right. I'm not even close to allowing myself to believe him one more time, when all my past attempts have only ended with my own heartbreak. But I'm not rigid enough not to acknowledge that he does seem to have changed. The Ben I knew all those years ago was all about what *he* wanted, when *he* wanted it. He never had enough patience to wait for anything, to play the long game. So, in that respect, I don't even recognize the man sitting in front of me.

The foolish, reckless, easily charmed part of me that loved him so desperately for so long wants to believe him. Wants to give him another shot just to feel the way I felt when I thought we were in love and together on the same page. Already he's chipping away at the resolve it took me so long to build up.

The waiter arrives with our food right as I open my mouth to say...I'm not even sure what I was going to say to what he just told me. I figure that's a sign - that maybe this is as good a time as any to take a step back and give myself some time to think about what's happening, about what he just told me. Maybe Ben *has* changed. It certainly seems that way, and I think Ben has proven himself enough so far that it's not just wishful thinking. He *is* different.

As we eat, we get caught up on each other's lives.

Ben fills me in on how his parents are doing, about how his company's softball team missed the playoffs by only a single point. He shows me pictures of the new apartment he just moved into, about trying his hand at some DIY projects during the remodel.

I ask him if he and Oliver still play frisbee in Central Park on Saturday mornings like a couple of frat boys. Back in college, I'd always wake up to an empty bed on the weekend mornings, and could usually find Ben there.

He laughs, tells me that they've graduated to talking about the stock market over breakfast after running a few miles on the treadmill. I tell him about Corinne (seems like Felicity has kept him updated on her life), about my site and branding efforts, about the book I've been reading before bed that I have difficulty putting down.

It feels comfortable, sharing things like this. Talking to him like we're old friends. This is what I was worried about, why I tried to keep things physical between us. My relationship with Ben has always been dichotomous. Fiery and full of passion, but comfortable, like a warm sweater on a cold winter night.

It's a dangerous combination.

"I'll have to buy that book," he says, finishing off the last bit of steak that was left on his plate.

"You should," I reply with a smile. "It's just your speed."

"When they inevitably make a movie out of it, maybe we could go together," he says tentatively. He's testing the waters.

I grin. The prospect isn't as unsavory as it would've been before. The more time I spend with him, the more time I want to spend with him. I want to know more about him, more about what makes him tick now that he's older. It's scary and exhilarating, like standing on a ledge that I've fallen off of so many times before, but knowing I have the strength to stay upright this time.

"Maybe we could."

He grins, and that's worth any of the lingering doubt or nervousness I feel at the answer.

"Not to push my luck here," he says, leaning forward. My heart starts beating double time. "But Caleb's become quite the cook lately, and he's having a barbecue this weekend. Mia mentioned meeting you at the fundraiser, and she really liked you. She and Caleb both want you to come, and I'm extending the invitation."

"Like a date?" I ask warily.

Ben shrugs. "That depends on you, Marisa. I want to date you, but I know you're not ready to give me that chance. So, this could just be two friends going to dinner at another friend's house, if that's something you're more comfortable with right now."

"I think I'd like to go to dinner with a friend." I catch the disappointment for a split second, and...god help me. "For now."

He perks right up at that, his eyes so bright and earnest and unbelieving. "For now?"

I'm not going to commit to anything yet, but I find myself more willing today than I was yesterday. Not totally willing, but...able to be swayed, at least.

"For now."

His responding smile is brighter than the sun.

CHAPTER
Nine

E ven though it's not a scenario that my mind would've ever dreamed up, sitting around the table with Ben, Caleb, and Oliver makes me feel oddly nostalgic. The last time we were all together like this was my last year in college, and the cracks in my relationship with Ben were already too large to fill.

Caleb's settling down, and Ben...well, it seems like maybe he's on the verge of wanting to do that, too. Oliver's the loner he's always been. Mia is here with us, and so is Felicity. There's an easiness and familiarity to our conversation, to just being together in the same place, that takes me by surprise. I can't quite pinpoint why that is, though.

We're at Caleb and Mia's apartment, the remnants of some perfectly grilled steaks and veggies on our plates. Our bellies are full, and we're laughing at a story Caleb is telling us about a trip he and Mia took to the farmer's market this morning.

I've been here for hours, and it still floors me just how much five years has changed Caleb. I never could've imagined the guy I knew back in college living with someone like Mia, looking at her the way he does, talking about going to the farmer's market like it's one of his favorite things. It's like one day we were all a bunch of college kids, and then I blinked and we were suddenly adults.

It makes me wonder if Ben really is serious about giving things another go. Trying to have an honest, adult relationship with me; one that's not based on lies and full of infidelity.

Ben is sitting next to me, nursing a glass of wine. He's wearing a dark-blue cotton shirt with the sleeves rolled up, giving me a nice view of his ridiculously muscular forearms. He's relaxed, comfortable in a way that he hasn't been when it's just the two of us together. Maybe that has something to do with the conversation we had yesterday. All the stress of *wanting* is gone now that he's finally put himself out there.

Ben's arm brushes mine every time he takes a sip of his red, and it sends shivers down my spine. He's not playing fair, even though I'm not sure that he's actually playing this time around. Maybe he's not trying to turn me on and is managing to do it anyway, just being himself. Of course, when I look at the muscles on his forearm tighten, all I can think of is the way they look when he's holding himself above me in bed, his body pressed to mine, making me see stars.

More laughter pulls me out of my little fantasy, and I join

in, not really sure what exactly is so funny. I missed whatever the punchline was, too busy fantasizing about Ben, which is just like old times.

Ben turns and gives me a curious look, like he recognizes that my laugh isn't real, and he wants to make sure that everything is okay.

I just smile.

"Needless to say, we forgot the celery," Mia says, giggling.

"Ugh, celery," Ben and I say in unison. We both look at each other, a little startled, a little wistful. Our hatred of that foul vegetable was one of the first things we bonded over when we first met.

I grin as I say, "Ninety-five percent water."

"Five percent evil," Ben finishes.

This red-hot blush creeps up, probably working its way up from my frantically beating heart. Ben and I must be looking at each other like a couple of fools, because everyone at the table is watching us.

I clear my throat and give my head a little shake to bring myself back into the moment.

"So, Caleb," I say, hoping a new line of conversation will turn the attention away from us. "I didn't know you liked to cook; I remember ramen being your specialty back in the day."

"That or ordering in," Ben teases.

"Is this a new thing?" I ask.

"Fairly new," he says, looking over at Mia. "I got tired of

waiting for takeout, and figured I should at least be able to make *something*. It kind of grew from there."

"Grew from there," Felicity mimics, laughing. "Didn't you want to go up to Maine this summer for private lessons at some farmhouse?"

I can't tell if Caleb is pretending to be offended, or if he actually is. "That was going to be a group vacation, and we were going to do other stuff!"

"What kind of other stuff?" Oliver asks.

"Crabbing, sailing. You know, summer things."

"The most WASPy summer ever," Felicity teases. She brings her glass of wine up to her lips, and I catch Oliver smiling at her like she's pure sunshine.

"No it isn't," Caleb replies defensively.

"Marisa." Felicity looks over at me. "You and your family spent every summer in Maine, didn't you? I remember Corinne telling me about it. Please, *please* let Caleb know the level of WASP we're talking about here."

"Felicity," Ben warns, leveling her with a glare that only a brother can.

I did spend every summer in Maine with my family, Felicity is right about that. We stayed in my grandmother's cabin, which my dad inherited when she died. My parents used it as a vacation home. A vacation home that they remodeled with money they stole from other people.

I look over at Ben, surprised that he even remembers

63

any of that. The house, the way that we got it. I feel a rush of affection for him for knowing that this is a sore spot for me.

Since I've rightfully been so standoffish about his advances since he showed up at my doorstep that night nearly a month ago, I figure I should also acknowledge the little moments like these, when he gives me a glimpse at the kind of person he is now, so completely different from the person he used to be.

I reach over and give Ben's arm a gentle squeeze, then offer him a smile.

"I did. And I'm sorry to tell you this, Caleb, but it's incredibly WASPy. You need cardigans, lots of cardigans. And pack plenty of boat shoes."

Caleb glares at me, then shoots a pleading look in Mia's direction. "She's exaggerating."

"I'm not," I tease. "It's exactly like that."

"Babe." Mia covers Caleb's hand with her smaller one. "We're going to have to talk about this."

When we've finished eating, and we're all talked out, Caleb starts taking the dishes back inside, insisting on cleaning up despite several offers from each of us to help. Mia is inside helping him. Ben and Felicity are over on the other side of the patio having some kind of disagreement, so I lean against the thick, ornate concrete railing, enjoying the gorgeous view.

The sun is setting, there's a light breeze, and we're far

enough up that the city seems almost quiet and serene. Living in a brownstone, much, much closer to the ground, it's not very often that I get to see New York's skyline from this point of view. When you spend your day on crowded sidewalks, weaving in and out of pedestrian traffic, it's so easy to forget how breathtaking this city can be.

"Hey," Oliver says, mirroring my pose as he rests his forearms against the concrete. He gives me a warm smile. It's the first time that we've spoken one-on-one besides a quick hug that he gave me when Ben and I first arrived.

"Hey."

He takes a swig of the beer he's holding, then playfully bumps his shoulder against mine. "It's good to have you back," he says earnestly. "I didn't realize how much I missed having you around, until you weren't anymore."

I push my hair behind my ear, and smile at the ground. Oliver has always been incredibly nice to me. Even back when Ben and I were dating, whenever he was acting like a shit head (which was often), I could always count on Oliver to offer me a sympathetic ear or a shoulder to cry on.

"I'm not sure I'm staying," I reply honestly.

He gives me a long, appraising look, and says, "You're staying."

The gall of Oliver's answer angers me, sets my entire body on edge. A moment ago I would've teased him, but I'm feeling indignant now.

CASSIE CROSS

"What makes you so sure?"

Oliver seems completely unfazed by the change in my attitude, he just looks over his shoulder to where Ben and Felicity are still having their heated little argument. His eyes linger on Felicity, like he thinks I won't notice, the lovesick idiot.

"He's different now," Oliver says, turning to me. "He's changed."

I let out a frustrated sigh. Where were all of these people fighting on my behalf back when Ben was still treating me like shit?

Like he can read my mind, he says, "We were on your side back when he was being a jackass. Trust me, I wouldn't lie to you about this. You'll see."

I give him a skeptical look, because I'm not sure that I believe him. I want to, but I'm not sure that I do. That I *can*.

"He loves you, Marisa," Oliver says. "He never stopped. It's just that now that he's grown up a little and understands what all of it means, he's not trying to run away. Not like he was back when you guys were together."

The sentiment is probably not as comforting as it should be.

"That's what he was doing before? Fucking other women because he loved me so much?" The idea of it is so ludicrous that I can't help but laugh.

"No," Oliver sighs. "You scared him that much. The

66

difference is that he's not scared anymore."

Ben said as much, but this coming from Oliver definitely gives me some more information to chew on while I figure out exactly what I'm going to do about whatever feelings I still have for Ben. There's no use in trying to deny that they're not there. They are. Now *I'm* the one who's scared. Rightfully so, I think.

For no other reason than because the opportunity has presented itself, I take my chance to turn the tables on Oliver.

"What about that?" I ask, nodding toward Felicity. "That scare you?"

Oliver gives me a very sad, resigned smile. "It doesn't matter. Nothing is going to happen there anyway."

"Why not?"

"I'm no good for her." God, I can tell that he actually believes that, and the thought of it is almost crushing. "Besides, Ben would beat my ass if I got involved with his sister, and I'd let him."

"Ignoring the fact that you are *so* wrong about not being good for her, Ben doesn't make decisions for Felicity," I tell him. "Or for you, last I checked."

Oliver presses his lips together, and looks out over the skyline, like he's actually considering what I've told him.

He takes a deep breath and says, "I can't. It's...it's not a good idea."

"Who's the scared one now?" I tease, bumping his shoulder

with mine.

A long silence stretches between us as Oliver absorbs what I said.

"I'm sorry about what happened with your parents," he finally says. "Well, about how it's affected you, at least. I can't say I'm sorry they got caught."

"Thank you."

"And I'm sorry that I couldn't make the benefit."

"I was only after your money, anyway," I tease. "Money that you so generously donated, so thank you for that."

He smiles at me. "Anytime. How's Corinne doing?"

"She's doing well. You know she's strong."

"Yeah," Oliver says, tapping the bottom of his beer bottle against the railing. "You Blake women are pretty resilient."

Ben offers me a ride home, sparing me what would probably be a never-ending cab ride. We chat about unimportant things in the back of his car as his driver weaves through the busy city traffic. When we pull to a stop in front of my brownstone, I invite Ben up against my better judgment.

He's been so sweet and attentive all day, and I'm too worked up from being around him for hours on end to go to bed unsatisfied. Why should I, when Ben is perfectly willing to take care of that for me, and does an incredible job of it, too.

It seems like Ben is feeling just as unsatisfied, because he's too impatient to wait for me to get my front door open. Once I turn the key in the lock, he has me pinned up against the door, his mouth hot and wanting, insistent against mine.

Somehow I manage to turn the doorknob, and the two of us stumble inside, our hands fumbling beneath each other's clothing to touch any stretch of skin they can reach.

Once we're safely inside, Ben moves us so my back is against the wall. While he's kissing, and licking, and sucking on my neck, he rucks up the skirt of my dress, then slides his hand beneath the waistband of my panties.

His fingers go right to my center, and I grind against his palm as his hand starts working its magic.

"This dress has been killing me all day," he says. His voice is all rugged and deep, full of want and desire.

"Yeah?" I whimper, as I fumble with the buttons on his shirt, wanting my mouth on his chest *immediately*.

"Mmm," he replies, flicking his fingers inside of me. "I've been looking at your legs all night, wanting them wrapped around me. Sitting next to you at dinner was torture. Every time your arm brushed against mine, I wanted to pull you into another room."

"To do what?" I ask, even though I know the answer.

He gets my arm free of one of my shoulder straps, then pulls my dress down and exposes my breast. He sucks on my nipple for a moment before he says, "To fuck you."

I let out this breathy moan, I can't help myself. He's never really been the kind of guy who talks a whole lot during sex, but when he does, and when it's filthy, it kicks me into overdrive.

"Why didn't you?"

"Because I knew you'd be loud, and I didn't want you to hold back," he says, giving my breast a little pinch. "Not with me."

I arch my back, wanting every bit of my body to be touching him, hoping I can make that happen.

"Wrap your arms around my neck," he says. His eyes are boring into mine, frantic with lust.

I do as he asks. He picks me up, and walks me over to the table on the other side of foyer. There's barely enough room for me on it given all the bric-a-brac on top of it, but I don't care about that stuff at this point.

As if he's just realizing that we don't have any room, he says, "Shit, let's…" He's looking around for somewhere else to go, and I don't even care where he fucks me as long as he does it *now*.

"Just…get rid of it," I say, my mouth close to his ear. I drag his lobe between my teeth, which makes him give my ass a squeeze. "Push everything off. Break it, I don't care."

Bless him, he looks even more excited at the thought of demolition sex, and a laugh breaks through the haze of lust that's taking over, because he's such a *guy*.

"Do it," I say.

He does. Mail is flying, glass figurines are bouncing across the floor, and I just don't care. He sets me down, and I'm working on the button on his jeans, my hands shaking as I fiddle with the zipper. I reach into his back pocket, and pull out his wallet, then find a condom tucked in next to a twenty. I rip the packet open with my teeth, then wait for him to shrug out of his boxer briefs before I roll the condom onto him.

After I spread my legs for him, I grip the fabric of his shirt between my fingers and pull. I never quite managed to get it all the way off, and that's working in my favor right now. Then, I say the words that I know will send him right over the precarious edge he's walking along. The point of no return.

"Fuck me."

He growls—actually *growls*—as he pushes inside me. We kiss frantically as he pounds into me, making the table's drawers clatter and clang as it bangs against the wall. Ben is sucking on my neck, his thumb working my clit, and I hang onto him for dear life as I come, burying my face against his shoulder.

His body stiffens, and he pulses inside of me with a long, low groan.

As we come down from our highs, breathing heavily, we both hang onto each other for dear life. In my blissed-out, hopeful, post-orgasmic haze, I find myself hoping like hell that everything he's been telling me is true.

I think I'm too far gone now to keep pushing him away.

I'm not sure I want to anymore.

CHAPTER
Ten

I wake up to the gentle tickle of Ben running his finger up and down my side, a pillow crushed under his arm, and he's cradling his head in his hand as he sleepily grins down at me.

"Hi," he says, his voice all sexy and morning-rough.

"Hi." I reply with a smile that I can't seem to help, and I brace my hands against the headboard, stretching out my tired muscles. They ache in the best way, from the best kind of overuse.

After once in the foyer, we made it to the steps before the next round, and then tested out the sturdiness off my bed and dresser a couple of times. It was mind-blowingly amazing. Like, better than it had ever been between us.

So, I'm happy, and feeling a little bit dazed this morning.

"I'm thinking about pancakes," Ben says, his fingers still

moving, finding their way along the curve of my breast, his thumb brushing over my nipple.

I let out a surprised laugh, and pretend like I'm offended (I'm just a little offended). "You've got your hand on my breast, and you're thinking about pancakes?"

His eyes widen in unbridled panic, and unfortunately for me, he removes his hand from where it was, stopping the very pleasant ministrations in the process.

"No! I didn't mean it like that, it's just…"

As he's in the middle of his explanation, his stomach rumbles, loud and clear.

Ben slides his hand along the underside of my breast now, and gives me a sly grin. "What I meant was that I worked up quite the appetite last night-"

"And this morning," I interrupt.

"Yeah." His thumb cuts across my nipple again, and I let out a soft little gasp. "And I was thinking about refueling with some pancakes."

Last night I took a step that I had been fighting for weeks, and now the two of us are in bed together on a Sunday morning, like we're a couple again, no cares in the world.

I've spent so long thinking that this couldn't happen again, swearing that I wouldn't *let* it happen again, that it almost feels impossible that Ben's here in bed with me, sharing this quiet intimacy as we tease each other about what we're going to have for breakfast.

Here, in the warm light of the early morning, so many things seem possible.

I just hope I won't wind up regretting this.

"I didn't come home with you to have sex with you. Just so you know."

I raise my brow, trying to look serious despite that pretty amazing thing he's doing with his hand. "Is that particularly important now? After all the sex we had, I mean."

"It's incredibly important," he says solemnly. "I just don't want you to think that, I don't know…that I took advantage of you."

It's almost unnerving to see him being so bashful now, but it's endearing as well. "I remember being a pretty enthusiastic participant. Multiple times."

He nods, and his stubble scratches against my forehead. "Yeah. I just wanted to make sure."

"Four orgasms later, you have one very satisfied customer."

Ben laughs, and the short huff of air blows a piece of hair across my forehead. It tickles, but I don't dare move. Lying here with him like this is perfect, I don't want to disturb it. But, I *am* curious.

"If you didn't come over here for sex," I say, sliding my hand across his broad, ridiculously muscled shoulder, "what did you come over here for?"

With an innocent shrug, Ben says, "You asked me to come up, and I just wanted to spend more time with you."

It's a good thing I'm lying down, because this man knows how make a girl a little weak in the knees. It's not exactly a new thing, the pillow talk. He's always been fairly good at seducing me, even back when he was a constant cheat. He can mess up a relationship for sure, but he also knows the right thing to say to get me going again. It can be a little unnerving to hear these things when I don't totally trust him, but I believe what he's telling me.

I know he's being sincere.

"I'm glad you did."

I can practically see the spark of hope that lights up his eyes. "Really?"

I nod.

"Is that you or your orgasms talking?"

A delighted laugh makes its way out of me. "Both?"

With a smile, Ben says, "I'll take it."

"There is one thing that I need to say, though."

Ben inhales a long, unsteady breath. "Okay."

I take his hand, so he doesn't think I'm about to drop a bomb on him, or break his heart or something. "If we're going to do this, if I agree to give you another chance…Ben, I swear to god if I catch you cheating on me again, I'll…" I can't even finish the thought. "I'm doing this against my better judgment, but I want to give you another chance. I want to give you the benefit of the doubt, that you've changed and you're a better person, and can be a better boyfriend than you were before.

Please don't make me regret that decision."

He cups my face in his hands, his eyes earnest as he leans down and gives me a soft kiss. "I won't make you regret it, I promise. I know my promises didn't mean much before, but they mean something now. You won't regret this."

"Okay," I breathe. "Okay."

He kisses me again, all slow and tender, and my mind gets going again, distracting me. I just have to say one more thing before we can move on.

"I do have a condition, though."

He nods without an ounce of hesitation. "Anything."

"I lose all sense of reason whenever I'm around you. It's like my brain is a lust-filled pile of mush. If we're going to do this, we're going to do it the right way."

He looks a little confused.

"I need to enter into this relationship with a level head. And the only way I can do that is if we take it slow. Be...I don't know, old-fashioned."

Ben's eyebrows scrunch together adorably. "What's old-fashioned?"

"You're going to take me on a date, and if I have a good time on that date, then you can ask me for another one."

"You...you want me to woo you?" Ben seems amused and...intrigued.

"Yes," I say shyly, even though I'm the one who brought up this whole thing.

"Okay. I will absolutely woo you. Consider it done. Is that it?"

"No." I slide my hand across his pec, relishing in the feel of it one last time…for a while. "There's another part, and you're not going to like that other part."

"What part is that?"

"The part where you're going to woo me, and while you're wooing me, we're not going to have sex. You're going to have to work for it." Taking sex off of the table is crazy, but it's the only way I know I can keep a level head here. I *need* to keep a level head for a little while.

"Okay," he says reluctantly. "On two conditions."

I'm interested. "What are those conditions?"

"I'd like our first date to be this morning. I'll take you to that diner down on Broadway that you like, and we'll get pancakes and bacon, and two carafes of that orange juice."

I enthusiastically agree to that condition. "Done. What's the other one?"

With a sly grin, Ben's hand slides down my belly, and between my thighs. He swipes his fingers along my slit, circling my clit with his thumb. It's like a power button for my whole body. Every part of me wakes up. Without giving it much thought, acting purely on instinct, I buck my hips against his hand.

"One more time. That's my second condition."

He's giving me this intense look, like all he wants is to live in this moment just a little while longer, like everything in his world is hinging on my answer. I gently push him until he's on his back, and I bring myself up on my knees, then straddle his hips. I grind down on him, making his back arch off the bed, his breath coming in short puffs. His hands reach up to cradle my breasts.

I'm already *loving* this condition.

"Okay," I say. "One more time." I scrape my fingernails across his abs, making his muscles flex and tighten. "But you better put your back into it."

CHAPTER
Eleven

A t a diner that's not too far away from my apartment, Ben and I are sitting across from each other at a small circular table, a carafe of orange juice between us, and half-eaten stacks of pancakes on both of our plates.

The fingers on my left hand are laced together with the fingers on his right, and we're leaning toward each other like a couple of magnets, even while we're eating. Ben reached out to take my hand when we first sat down, and we haven't let go since. I was hesitant at first, but when he looked at me with those eyes that always manage to make me feel a little weak in the knees, I couldn't help but oblige him.

Ben runs the pad of his thumb over my knuckles, back and forth, and the sensation is endlessly soothing.

"What do you have planned for the rest of the day?" he asks, as he reaches for his glass of juice.

I close my eyes for a second, mentally running through all of the appointments that I know are filling up my calendar, even though it's a weekend.

"I have a conference call with a designer in Paris who wants to use my site to launch a new line. After that, I have a meeting with some developers who are hopefully going to get to work on some new features that I want to add to the navigation bar."

Ben squeezes my hand. "I can do that for you, you know. For free."

I'm not worried about the money, and the gesture is sweet, but I can't take him up on his offer. It's a bad idea on pretty much every level. Instead of flat-out turning him down, I decide to go with another argument first.

"You're a software engineer, not a web developer," I say, as I slide the tines of my fork through a puddle of syrup, swiping it across my plate into what I think is a pretty elegant design. I need to do whatever I can to avoid the look in his eyes when he starts to convince me that I should let him do the work for me anyway.

"I can do both," he says.

Yeah, I didn't think that argument was going to work for me, but it was worth a try anyway. I take a deep breath, and give myself a moment to figure out a way to frame this argument that isn't going to make him fight me against it more, and isn't going to hurt his feelings.

"I…I would prefer to keep my business life and my personal life separate." I've got a great team of developers that I have a great relationship with, and I don't want to chance burning those bridges just so I can start relying on Ben for something that will be taken away if things don't work out between us this go 'round. I'm hoping this short answer is enough, so I won't have to explain myself.

He nods reluctantly. "I get it. But if you ever need a quick fix and can't get them on the phone for whatever reason, I'm always here for you."

I can't help but smile at him. "I know." I believe him now, whether or not I should.

"So," I say, because even though he relented, he still sounds disappointed, and I don't like hearing that tone in his voice. Especially not when I'm the one who put it there. "This has been a pretty good date thus far."

He gives me a thoughtful look. "I'm not sure that I want this to be a first date."

I tilt my head. "What do you mean?"

Ben shrugs. "Even though we had a ton of shitty memories from our previous…"

"Tries?" I offer.

"Okay, tries. Even though we had some bad memories from those, we had some really good ones. Memories that I don't want wiped away just because we're trying to start over."

Him admitting that gives me a warm feeling, and I can

see where he's coming from. It wasn't all bad between us, we definitely had some good in there.

"Okay." I smile.

"This is a good date though, no matter which number it is. I mean, I'm having a good time. I have you, I have pancakes. All I need."

He's excellent at this wooing stuff.

"I went all out for you, as you can see," I say, motioning toward the mess that is my ensemble with an ironically elegant flourish. My hair is piled up on top of my head in the messiest bun imaginable, and I'm wearing an old pullover paired with yoga pants that have definitely seen better days. I don't have any makeup on, but I do have the post-coital glow that only comes from orgasm after orgasm, so I've got that going for me, I guess.

Ben untangles his fingers from mine, then reaches over and cups my cheek with his hand. "You're beautiful, and this is all I need."

"You and me and breakfast food," I tease, trying to cover up the way the soft touch of his hand makes me shiver. I place my hand over the back of his, then turn my head and kiss his palm.

I know he's told me that things are different now, and he's shown me glimpses of it for sure, but this *feels* different. Old Ben would have showered me with expensive things, would've taken me to the hippest restaurant in town (and he could've this time, he's the co-owner of one of them). This—the two of us, uncomplicated—was all I ever wanted.

And now, here, I have it.

I'm *happy*.

"So, it's been a while since we met, and I'm wondering if anything has changed." With the way he's grinning, I'm sure he's playing with me, but I'm willing to play right back. "Tell me a little about yourself."

"Hmmm," I say, tapping my finger against my chin. "Well, I'm twenty seven, and I like long walks on the beach, love the way the sand feels between my toes." I do my best impression of a contestant on a cheesy dating game show, because Ben already knows all of the things about me that really matter. "I like watching the sun set over the city, and chocolate ice cream is my weakness."

Thoroughly amused, Ben leans forward, close enough so that only I can hear him. "I can think of a few things I'd like to do with that chocolate ice cream."

I give his arm a playful smack. "I told you not even two hours ago that if we're going to do this that *doing things* with chocolate ice cream is strictly off-limits for the foreseeable future. You're supposed to be wooing me."

"What, I can't woo you with a list of ways I'd like to lick that ice cream off of your body?"

Oh, imposing a no-sex rule on this is going to be the end of me, I can feel it.

"Why don't you tell me a little bit about yourself?" I'm basically opening the door for him to get dirty again, so this is a dangerous road for us to travel down if he's not going to stay on message.

"Let's see…I'm twenty eight, and I still have my very first video game console. I'm remodeling my apartment, and learning to lay tile, because I figure it's good to know how to do that kind of a thing. I always thought it was easy. It looked easy, at least. I took for granted that it would be a piece of cake for me, but now I'm realizing how easy it is to screw up. So, I'm learning."

It's impossible for me to miss the double meaning there.

Ben pulls my hand up to his lips, and presses a kiss against my fingers.

We finish our meal, and after Ben pays the check, we walk out of the diner. Ben's arm is around my shoulder, and mine is around his waist. He pulls me in close, presses a kiss against my temple. I smile, and turn to look across the street, where I'm almost certain that I see someone hidden in a car, with a telephoto lens pointed at us. It's something that I've gotten used to since my parents' scandal broke, and it's not like I can do anything about it, so I just turn back into Ben's embrace, and try to forget about the outside world for a while.

Ben and I separate two blocks away from my apartment,

because I need to make a stop at a specialty store to pick up some ingredients that I'm going to use for some baking that I'm planning on doing later. He's reluctant to go, but he's supposed to meet Felicity later on this morning. Before we part, Ben pulls me behind a small pillar decorating the side of a building, giving us a little privacy from the foot traffic on the sidewalk.

With one hand rooted to the concrete, and the other on my hip, he gives me a long, lingering goodbye kiss. His soft touches are electric, even just the feeling of his fingertips brushing across my cheeks. This is new, but it's not. It's familiar, but thrilling.

I'm determined not to talk myself out of this feeling, though. I'm going to bask in it, and not worry about the other shoe dropping.

As he walks away toward his awaiting car, he turns and looks at me every few steps, then gives up on that completely, walking backwards so he can keep his eyes on me. I laugh at him, and am wearing a smile so big that it actually hurts my face. Somehow, the goofy wave that he gives me when he gets into the car makes that smile even bigger.

I feel like I'm floating all through the market, and when I return home with my purchases, I'm still riding high as I set my bag down to unlock my door.

Then a chill washes over all that bliss when I see someone walk up behind me in the reflection of the glass panels on the door. I do my best not to acknowledge that I've even seen him, and instead reach into my cross-body bag to find my pepper spray.

"You won't need it," says the man behind me. He follows that up with an incredibly creepy, "Miss Blake."

Because I don't know what else to do right now, and because I stupidly decided to forego the security detail that my lawyer—Nancy—suggested that I hire, I try to scare him a little.

"I have mace, and there is surveillance on this property," I say without even turning around. Both of these things are true, although what good they'll do me? I have no idea. My heart his pounding, fear and adrenaline rushing through my veins. "So think long and hard about what you're going to do before you do it."

I can see what looks like a smile in the glass door pane.

"I'm not here to hurt you. But it is in your best interests to speak to me. And you're going to do what I tell you."

I figure maybe this is a reporter trying a new tactic to get me to talk to him, when I haven't been willing to talk to anyone else.

"I don't have any comments on my parents' case. Nothing you say to me is going to change that."

Then, another chilling thought comes over me. What if this isn't someone who wants me to comment on the case, what if it's someone they stole from? What if it's someone here to collect on their debt? Yet again, in the span of two minutes, I'm left wondering what in the hell I was thinking turning down that security detail. It seemed like a ridiculous notion at the time, and I had wanted to seem independent and unaffected, but everything about that seems incredibly stupid now, faced with this crippling fear.

"Turn around," he says with authority. "We're standing in public, Marisa. I'm not going to hurt you here."

Meaning…maybe he *would* hurt me if we were somewhere else. Can't let myself think about that, though. It's not going to get me through this confrontation.

I look to my left, and to my right, hoping that Ben had a change of heart, or just wanted to come back for another kiss, but sadly, there's no sign of him. Or anyone else, for that matter. Great.

"What do you want?"

"I want you to do something for me."

I let out an unladylike snort. "No."

"Trust me," he says, his voice low. "When you see this, you'll do it."

It's dangerous and stupid, but my curiosity gets the better of me, and I turn around. I'm hit with a spark of familiarity from him, but he's difficult to recognize under the baseball cap and sunglasses he's wearing. But he's definitely young - he can't be much older than I am, and despite the disguise, he's nicely dressed. He doesn't look like an investigative reporter, so I'm not sure what he could possibly want. Nothing good, though, that's for sure.

"What is it that you want from me?" I ask.

"Take a look," he says, handing me a large, thick envelope.

Without giving it much thought, I gently take the envelope from him, almost painfully curious about what's inside. I've never been served before, but I don't think this is how it goes. This must be something else.

"You've been seeing Ben Williams again."

The "again" strikes me as odd, but given the whole situation at the moment, I'm not going to call him out on that. I'm guessing he was the one in the car with the camera pointed at us when we left the diner? God, I wish I had the sense to take down the vehicle's license plate number.

I suppose it doesn't really matter that he knows.

"I haven't been keeping that a secret." There hasn't been much of a secret to keep, and we haven't even seen that much of each other, really. Unless this man has been watching my home.

"I want something from him, and you're going to get it for me."

I laugh at his gall. "No, I'm not."

"Open that envelope." He nods at my hands.

I do as he says, out of nothing more than panicked curiosity. My fingers tremble as I pull up the prongs keeping it fastened, then I look inside and see the edges of what has to be photo paper. Shit. A feeling of dread washes over me as I reach inside and pull them out.

Tears spring to my eyes when I see what is on them. Picture after picture that I'm having difficulty even holding onto; all the strength in my body drains a little more with every snapshot I look at. It's a violation. It's disgusting, and illegal, and…

"How did you even get these?" I ask, voice trembling.

Picture after picture of my sister, naked and having sex with some man whose face I can't even make out. Was he in on this? My stomach rolls as I put the pictures back in the envelope. I've seen enough.

"Bodyguards can't protect her from a telephoto lens, Marisa."

"You son of a bitch," I say. I consider slapping him, but my arms won't move. I'm just…frozen.

He gives me this evil grin, like he can read my mind. "You don't want to mess with the person who has a digital file of those pictures."

"What are you going to do with them?" I try to keep my voice steady, because I don't want this man to know how scared I am, but I fail spectacularly.

He shrugs. "That depends on what you're willing to do for me."

"Who are you?"

"That's not really any of your concern," he says with a

laugh. "It's definitely not relevant to this transaction."

"What's the transaction?" I ask, desperation coloring my voice. "Do you want money?" This asshole can have every last cent in my bank account if he agrees not to release these pictures.

"No," he says, long and drawn out. "All the money in the world couldn't get you out of this. I want something that money can't buy. Not yet, at least."

"What is it?" I ask, rapidly losing my patience.

"Your boyfriend Mister Williams is developing a software that I am incredibly interested in. So interested, in fact, that I'm going to release these pictures of your sister to every website, every tabloid, if you don't get it for me."

I don't think this man even knows what he's asking. I don't know the first thing about computers, and I know for a fact that I couldn't get into Ben's computer to get this software even if I did. And it's not like I can just ask him for it.

"How am I supposed to do that?"

He shrugs. "That's not my concern. I've left a thumb drive and a card with my information on it in that folder. You have a week, Miss Blake."

With that, he has the nerve to tip his hat at me. "Oh," he says, like he's remembered something important. "I'll be watching you, so…watch yourself." Then he turns and walks away.

Belatedly, I realize that I should've followed him, but I'm

too stunned and scared to move. Eventually, and with great effort, I manage to get my door unlocked. I make it just inside, bolt the lock, then lean against the wall, and slide down to the floor, the pictures in my hands. I want to destroy them, to watch them burn, but I don't. Maybe there's something inside that could help me figure out who this man is, and who took these pictures.

I find the thumb drive, and pull out the business card, which contains only a phone number. On the back is the project name of the program he wants me to steal. RV-7.

I want to throw up.

What should I do? This man has obviously been watching me. Will he know if I tell Ben what happened? Do I dare risk it? How could I betray Ben after being angry at him all these years for the way that he treated me? At least I wasn't blind to his behavior, I got what I was expecting. This? He would never expect that kind of betrayal from me. It would devastate him.

What's worse is that these pictures being released would devastate my sister. I don't want her to endure that, especially after everything she's gone through. If I make one wrong move, that man could release these pictures all over the internet with the simple push of a button.

I'm too scared to ask anyone for help, and I'm too scared to sleep.

I have no idea what I'm going to do.

CHAPTER
Twelve

The next evening, Ben and I are sitting together on a bench in a quiet, empty section of Central Park watching as the sun turns the sky a fiery orange and pink.

I've been keeping an anxious eye out for any movement around the park. I'm trying not to look paranoid, but when someone tells you that they've been watching you, it's kinda difficult *not* to be paranoid. Did he have surveillance around my house? Had he been listening to my conversations? I didn't know what or where was safe, and I was afraid to test the limits to find out. Maybe he didn't have any surveillance on me, and was trying to rattle me by throwing that out there.

Well…it worked.

So, I'm doing my best to enjoy the evening, without worrying too much about what happened yesterday. I'm failing miserably.

There's a picnic basket on the ground in front of the bench that Ben and I are sitting on. Earlier, the basket was filled with some food from my favorite gourmet shop. But now, our bellies are full, and we're drinking some fabulous wine. Ben's arm is around me, and his fingertips are lightly tracing circles on my upper arm.

I rest my head against his shoulder and cuddle into his side, enjoying the comfortable silence that the two of us have always been able to share.

We're both watching the runners that pass through every few minutes, the people walking their dogs, a family pushing their toddler in a stroller along the winding trails. The wind is blowing, cool, but not cold.

It's perfect.

Well, it would be perfect if someone hadn't blackmailed me into stealing from Ben in order to prevent pictures of my sister having sex being leaked to the world. I stayed awake all night trying to figure out what my next move would be, but I think I'm doing an excellent job of hiding that.

I'm so lost in my thoughts that I'm actually startled when Ben speaks.

"Are you going to tell me what's bothering you?"

I raise my head. "What?"

He gives me a look that lets me know that playing this off and pretending like something isn't wrong isn't going to work with him.

"I know you've got something on your mind. Are you going to tell me what it is?"

For the thousandth time since that man showed up on my front step yesterday, I wonder if I can just tell Ben. That's one of the nagging thoughts that kept me awake all last night. I know he'd try to help me. Hell, maybe he'd just give me the program outright. Okay, so…yeah, as a business woman myself, I know that's a pipe dream, but with this new version of Ben, I'm not sure that option is completely off the table.

I need to figure this out, and fast. I shouldn't even be here on this date right now, but I was worried that cancelling would tip Ben off that something was wrong, and this is one part of my life that has been going well lately. I didn't want to mess that up.

I can't steal from him. I *can't*.

Yet, I also can't let Corinne suffer if I make a wrong move.

"Marisa?"

His hand slides into mine, and our fingers twine together.

"If you don't want to tell me…if it's a trust thing, then I get it. I just want to be here for you."

"It's not that I don't trust you," I say quickly. That is absolutely the truth. I know I can trust him with this, I'm just worried about what will happen if the man who's watching me finds out that I told Ben what's going on. The cautious part of me wants to keep this wrapped up tight until I absolutely have to say something. "It's just that I'm not ready to talk about it right now."

"Is your business in trouble?" he asks, unable to let it go.

I shake my head.

"It's...it's not about your parents is it?" His voice is tentative.

I give him a sad smile. "No, that's not it."

"It isn't anything I can help you with?"

I shake my head again. "No, I don't think so."

He lets out a deep breath, looking a little helpless. I can tell that he wants to ask me more questions, but he knows me well enough to know that if I haven't answered him by now, I'm not going to answer him. I appreciate him noticing and caring, but I'm not sure what my next move should be right now. I've got a lot of experience with pretending like something terrible isn't bothering me (thanks, Mom and Dad!), so I need to put on my everything-is-right-with-the-world face already.

To distract Ben from his line of questioning, and to distract myself from my increasingly panicked and depressing thoughts, I lean in and give Ben a kiss.

"Mmm," he hums against my lips. "What was that for?"

Even with everything going on, I figure this is as good a time as any to start rewarding Ben for being a good boyfriend, if...well, if that's what he is.

"It's for noticing. For asking."

The corner of his mouth quirks up into an adorable smile, and I just have to kiss that, too.

"I'm going to have to notice and ask more often."

"That's generally advisable, even if you don't get kisses as a reward," I say lightly, even though there's an undercurrent of truth to the sentiment.

Ben re-corks the wine bottle, and puts it back in the picnic basket.

"This was a really good idea," I tell him.

"It was yours," he says, looking back at me with happy eyes.

"It was?" I ask, surprised. I don't remember ever having an idea like this. I love this park, sure, but it's more of a favorite of Ben's, and I know I haven't mentioned anything like this recently, at least.

"Yes," he says, settling back against the bench, and wrapping his arm around me again. "It was the night after we had that big fight down on Broadway, remember?" He smiles a little, kind of wistful. "It was one of the few arguments we had that wasn't…"

He trails off, and I'm curious about what he was going to say. I need him to finish that sentence. "One of the few arguments that wasn't what?"

"Nothing," he says. "That part isn't important."

"Okay. What's the important part?"

"We got tickets to that play you wanted to wanted to see, and-"

I take a deep breath and nod, because I remember exactly what he's talking about now. He was on his phone all night, just generally making sure that I knew that he didn't want to be there.

"I remember."

I left the theater in a huff at intermission, and he and I had argued about it loudly on the sidewalk, and drew some unwanted attention to ourselves. A couple of people had snapped pictures, and Ben's parents weren't very happy with us. Mine didn't really seem to care, probably because they were up to no good themselves.

"That wasn't a good night," I say, letting him off the hook for the rest of the story.

Ben swallows so hard that I can see his Adam's apple bobbing underneath the collar of his shirt.

"After we made up, we went back to my apartment, remember?"

I do remember the making up...*that* was a good night. "Yeah."

"We made love for hours, and after, we just talked. You promised that you'd never make me go to the theater again, and we talked about what our idea of a perfect date was. You said you thought it would be romantic to have a picnic in the park."

I smile, remembering that night. "Even youthful me was into the wooing."

Ben looks over at me with a hint of regret in his eyes. "And back then I couldn't be bothered to woo you. I want to make sure I do things right this time."

"You're doing them right," I assure him. Now, the person who's doing things wrong is me. The fact that I'm even considering doing what that man asked me to do is terrible on so many levels. I decided to trust Ben again after he betrayed me so many times, and here I am, enjoying a romantic picnic that he made for me, kissing him, wanting more, all the while secretly planning on doing something that will completely break his trust in me.

I don't want to think about that, though. I'll think about it later, when I'm home by myself, guilt-ridden about being such a shitty person, and worrying about what I'm going to do next.

Ben stands up, swipes some crumbs off of his pants, and holds his hand out to me.

A slow smile stretches my lips, and for a blissful second, I actually forget about what had me so worried in the first place. "What are you doing?"

"Dance with me."

"What?" I ask, with an amused laugh.

"Dance with me, Marisa." His voice is low and gravely, but his eyes are open and earnest. So, I can't help but do as he asks. I take his hand, and let him pull me up until my body is flush against his. His arms slide around my back, one hand venturing a little too low to be decent. I wrap my arms around his neck and rest my head against his chest, breathing in the clean, manly, *Ben* smell of him.

"We don't have any music," I whisper. My fingers stroke up the back of his neck, where they play with the hairs at the nape.

His fingers run a light circuit up and down my spine. He turns his head, his whiskers brushing my cheek, then he presses his lips against the shell of my ear.

"We don't need any music," he says, his warm breath making me shiver.

We start moving together in time to an imaginary beat, and I let myself melt into the warmth of Ben's embrace.

CHAPTER
Thirteen

"**W**hat do you think about this one?" Felicity asks, as she straightens out the skirt on a tall, blonde model standing in front of us. She's lanky and gorgeous, the perfect fit for the new fall line that an up-and-coming designer signed on with me to debut on my website.

I'd hired Felicity on again as a last-minute thing after my last conversation with Corinne. She was right about Felicity: she was responsible for styling one of the top-rated shoots on my site, and I figured that it would be foolish not to use her for something like this, especially since the reception of her work was so good last time.

It was a no-brainer for me, and for the designer.

Now that she's showing me the concept for the next sequence of photos, I'm not so sure.

"I like it, but I think we should do away with the wool

dress in the next sequence, if we're going with this here. Maybe put those printed pants on the taller model?"

Felicity steps back and gives the scene a thoughtful look, pursing her lips as she ponders my suggestion. "I like the aesthetic the way it is, and I think that keeping the dress in gives a better mix of styles, don't you think? That way they're not *all* in pants. Plus, the print on the dress works better with the background, in my opinion."

I don't necessarily agree with her opinion, but I'm paying her for her expertise, and that expertise has already paid off for me tenfold previously. So, I'm going to go along with her on this one, even if I don't agree with her.

"Okay," I say.

Felicity's eyes light up. "Yeah?"

"Yeah, let's go with your idea."

Felicity beams at me, like she's won a prize. Sometimes it's difficult to remember how young she is. She walks into a shoot, takes charge, and makes the room her own. Then she basks under a little bit of praise, and that youthful exuberance of hers just shines through the professional exterior.

She's always wanted approval, and I'm happy to give it to her here, especially when she's doing such great work.

"After this next series of shots are done, how about we break for lunch?"

Felicity nods. "Sounds good."

The shoot is catered, but I'd like to sneak away with her for a quick chat, and don't want to be disturbed if I can possibly help it.

"There's a place around the corner that has good salads," I suggest.

She smiles at me. "I'd like that."

Felicity and I manage to grab a couple of salads to go; the restaurant was way too crowded to be able to talk to her (and actually be able to hear her answers), which was the whole point of me asking her to lunch. We find a quiet corner of the studio to sit down and eat in.

As she's munching away on a forkful of lettuce, I say, "I'm going to ask you something, and I want you to be completely honest with me, even if you think that I won't want to hear the answer, okay?"

Felicity gives me a curious look, and I figure I better explain more about my motivation here before expecting her to agree.

"I'm not talking to you as your boss for the day," I say, dipping a tomato into some dressing. "I'm talking to you as a concerned sister."

Felicity takes a deep breath, and nods in acknowledgment. She sits rod straight, her eyes wide, probably afraid that I'm going to ask her to break the code of friendship or something.

"Okay," she says reluctantly.

"Is Corinne okay? I talk to her a couple times a week, and I think I'm pretty good at reading her. She seems like she's doing fine, but I know that you saw her just the other day, and you would know better than I would if she's dealing as well as she's saying she is."

Felicity puts down her fork, and looks at the ground.

"You don't have to tell me anything that you don't want to, or that Corinne has asked you not to. I'm not trying to pry, honestly. I'd like to go visit her, but she told me not to…I think she's worried that I'll hover, or that I'll never leave," I say with a nervous laugh. "I want to respect her wishes, but I also want to make sure that she isn't struggling more than she's letting on, and I'm just letting it slide and not helping her when she needs it."

What I really want to do is show her the photos that man gave me, and ask her if she knows who he is. But there aren't any shots of his face, and the security guy that's been looking out for her hadn't ever seen the man in the picture before. I didn't want to go so far as to post a guard outside of her apartment, so I had told the guy to give her some space. I'm regretting that now.

Plus, I can't ask about the guy without showing Felicity the picture, and if I do that, she'll tell Corinne. I don't want Corinne to worry about anything that she doesn't have to worry about. I'm going to take care of this, I just have to figure out…*how*.

"She's doing okay, Marisa." Felicity smiles, probably because she's felt the overbearing protectiveness of her brother several times throughout her life to know that even though we ask tough questions, we definitely mean well. "School is fine, she's going to graduate on time. Please don't worry about that. It's just…it's rough for her right now. There's gossip about her, and she's never been as confident as you are, so it's a little bit difficult for her to deal with all that. But she *is* dealing. She's doing okay. If you have some vision of her crying herself to sleep every night, well…it's nothing like that."

I have to smile at how well Felicity can read me. I definitely didn't think that Corinne was crying herself to sleep at night, but I did wonder if she was feeling a little lonely.

"Okay, thank you," I say, reaching over and giving her forearm a little reassuring squeeze.

"She's strong, and she's doing okay. She has a good role model to look up to."

I lean forward, curious. I want to know who this person is, so I can do a background check on them. I'm only partly kidding about that. I'm hoping she's going to tell me, but when she doesn't come out with a name, my curiosity gets the better of me.

"Who is it?"

Felicity's eyes narrow. "Who is who?"

"Corinne's role model."

Felicity rolls her eyes. "Are you serious right now?"

"Yes," I say slowly, not sure what she's so confused about.

"It's you, you idiot. I'm talking about you."

"Me?" I'm so stunned that it's difficult for me to even comprehend what she's talking about.

"Yes, you." She bumps my shoulder with hers.

I feel so much pride right now, that I think my chest might break apart from it. It makes me feel like something in this world is right after so many things have gone wrong, and it definitely drives me to do right by Corinne as far as these photos are concerned. I can't let her down. I just can't.

So I finish my lunch sitting across from the very sweet young woman whose brother I'm trying to figure out how to betray.

CHAPTER
Fourteen

Thanks to Felicity's efficiency, and the fact that I'm too lost in my own thoughts and anxiety to really debate about much, the shoot ends ahead of schedule. As a crew disassembles the sets, I sit in a flimsy director's chair in a shadowy corner of the studio, going over my options for about the thousandth time.

My leg is bouncing, and I'm gnawing on a raggedy thumbnail trying to figure out a scenario in which this whole thing works out well for Corinne.

I honestly can't think of a single one.

The fact of the matter is that I don't have the slightest clue about how to get that program from Ben, apart from outright asking for it. I'm scared to ask anyone for help, because what if this guy is watching me? What if that triggers a response?

Why would anyone come to someone like me with a task

like that? If you're that desperate to get something, wouldn't you go to a person with specialized skills who could actually get it for you? Maybe he knew I wouldn't be able to do it... maybe this was all just an exercise to wind me up until he inevitably releases the photos anyway.

I mean, the guy somehow got close enough to know about the project, so he had to either work for Ben or know someone who does, right? Every bit of headway that I think I make in figuring this out sends me into another tailspin of panic, of helplessness.

I don't know a way out of this, and sitting in the dark stewing on it isn't going to help me or Corinne. The closer I inch toward my week deadline, the more anxiety becomes my constant companion.

I'm not sleeping well, I can't stay focused on work, and my thoughts are increasingly funneling down into one pinpointed focus: those pictures, those pictures, those pictures.

I've got to get out of here, to do something, to get involved in some mindless task that can free up my mind for a few hours. Hell, I'd take a few *minutes* at this point.

About an hour later, I walk into Ben's office building, holding a bag from his favorite deli. He's working late tonight, so I figured I'd be a good girlfriend and make sure he eats.

All while I'm trying to figure out how to steal from him.

The thought makes my stomach roll, as I hand my ID to the guard in the lobby. I had called Ben's assistant and asked her to put my name on the list to get in, quietly hoping she'd somehow know what I was up to and deny me access.

The guard lets me in, of course, and I make my way up to his floor without having a breakdown. I step out into the workspace—it's the first time I've ever been here—and smile at all the ways it's just so...Ben. It's collaborative and fun. Employees are huddled around work tables, talking through their ideas, excited about the work that they're doing. He's surrounded himself with the kind of people who want to build him up, not tear him down.

People completely unlike me.

Ben's assistant lets me into his office, and asks me if I'd like a drink. I don't think they have enough alcohol in the world to dull the panic rising inside of me, so I gracefully decline. She tells me she has to run and make some copies, that Ben's in a meeting that's running long, and to push the red button on his phone if I need anything.

I give her my thanks, then walk over to Ben's desk. It's pretty clean; Ben—being the tech guy that he is—doesn't really work with a lot of papers. Seems like most of his files are electronic. There's a blue sticky note stuck to the corner of his monitor that catches my eye.

The name of the program I've been looking for is scribbled in Ben's messy handwriting.

A rush of manic excitement hits me square in the chest. This is my chance, the first chance I've had to get that program, and it presented itself completely by accident. I sit down at his desk, and pull the keyboard out of the drawer beneath the monitor.

With a jolt of the mouse, the screen comes to life.

The picture on the password screen is one he must've snuck of me while we were in the diner a few days ago, after I told him I wanted to give this another go. I look...content. I remember being happy, and it feels like that morning was years ago.

And here I am, frantically guessing passwords to try to break into his computer. It doesn't hit me until the third try that Ben's the kind of guy who would probably install a monitor to let him know when someone's entering incorrect passwords into his computer.

He's got this picture of me on his desktop, and he's trying to atone for the things that he did in the past, and I'm sitting here violating his privacy, trying to steal from him.

My hands are shaking, and I'm breaking out in a cold sweat. Just this morning Felicity told me that my baby sister looks up to me as a role model, and look at me now. God, how far I've fallen in the span of an afternoon.

What would she think of me now?

She and I completely cut our parents out of our lives when their scandal broke. I still remember the morning we found out that the people we'd loved and looked up to our whole lives weren't the people we thought they were at all. They were liars and thieves.

Just like me.

I don't want my sister's privacy to be violated, for her body and her life choices to be put out into the world for judgment by the masses. But can I become the kind of person I know she would hate to keep it from happening?

I think she would be ashamed of me right now. I know I'm ashamed of myself.

I slide off the chair and onto my knees as I clamor for the trash can that's to the left of Ben's desk. I barely pull it in front of me in time to retch into it, throwing up what little bit is in my stomach, and crying as I do it.

"Jesus, Marisa." Ben's panicked voice finds its way through the sound of my heartbeat pounding in my ears. He drops to his knees next to me and pulls my hair back, his other hand running soothingly up and down my spine. "Do I need to call a doctor? Are you okay?"

I'm crying, coughing, and generally a mess. The only thing I can do to communicate is give my head a pitiful shake.

"No," I manage, my voice weak. "I'm just…"

Not feeling well wouldn't quite cover it. What other way could I explain it? That it turns out that maybe I'm not such a great person after all, and maybe he should get away from me while he can? That would be closer to the truth.

Ben's secretary is standing by the doorway, her fingers fidgeting. "Should I call an ambulance?" she asks.

I shake my head vehemently. Absolutely no ambulances.

"No," Ben tells her. He asks her to bring me some tissues, and helps me wipe off my face when she does.

Once my stomach has settled and I'm a little less hysterical, Ben gently helps me to my feet, then picks me up. It's easy, like I weigh nothing.

Ben takes me to the ensuite bathroom in his office, and sets me down on top of the (covered) toilet. He turns on the faucet, then pulls a washcloth off of the top of a stack of fluffy white towels just outside of his shower. Despite what I've just gone through, somehow my mind drifts into frivolous thoughts, like how often someone comes in and replaces the towels.

Once the washcloth is wet to Ben's satisfaction, he kneels down in front of me, dabbing the cloth on my sweat-dampened skin. He lovingly pushes my hair back from my face, then cups my cheek.

"What's the matter?" he says, sounding comforting and concerned at the same time. "Are you going to keep telling me it's nothing, or are you going to be honest with me?"

I reach up and cover his hand with mine, twining our fingers together against my cheek. I take a deep breath and look at the floor, because I can't meet his eyes right now.

"I'm scared to tell you," I admit. I only manage to say that much because I'm emotionally exhausted and tired of keeping secrets. And because I feel so hopeless. There's no way I can do what I've been asked to do, but at the same time, how can I not?

I don't want to lie to Ben anymore. It's only been a few days; I can't imagine what kind of state I'll be in once my week is up, and I'm no closer to a solution than I am right now.

Ben reaches behind him and shuts the bathroom door.

"Why are you scared?" he asks. His voice is very calm and soft, but his body is all coiled up with tension. "Is someone scaring you? Are you being threatened?"

I lower my head, letting my hair create a curtain around me. I just want to hide from him right now. Hide from the world.

"Marisa," he says gently, as he crooks his fingers under my chin and lifts my head so that my eyes meet his. "Is somebody threatening you?"

His eyes are intense; I've never seen this look on him before, like there's a quiet storm raging inside, ready to go completely out of control depending on what answer I give him.

His jaw tightens, and his teeth are clenched. He asks again, less patient this time. "Is someone threatening you?"

I nod. "Yes."

The washcloth he was holding drops to the floor, and his hands clench up into fists, before they relax again. Tenderly, as if he wasn't just full of anger, he holds my face in his hands.

"Why were you scared? You know I would never let anybody hurt you."

I do know that. Even back when Ben was the one being irresponsible with my feelings, if anyone had dared to threaten me, he would've made them regret it.

"They aren't threatening to hurt *me*," I admit quietly. My voice is barely a whisper.

Ben looks surprised at that admission. "Who are they threatening?"

"Corinne."

CHAPTER
Fifteen

On the ride to Ben's apartment, he held my hand and let me stare out the window. He didn't press me for answers.

Now, we're sitting across from each other at his dining room table, and I know the questions are going to be coming soon.

"I talked to the head of my security team," he says quietly, even though I can hear the burning anger bleeding through his voice. "He's coming over."

I look up at him, and he must see the panic in my eyes.

"He's going to be discreet, Marisa. We don't have much time to nip this in the bud, but we're going to, okay?"

I nod.

The envelope with the pictures sits on the table between us. I've been carrying it around with me, which I realize now wasn't a smart move, but I didn't want to leave them lying around where anyone could find them. I didn't want to burn or shred them in case I decided to ask for some help with this; I figured there could be some identifying information on the envelope or photos.

Turns out that was the right decision.

"I was going to steal from you," I blurt out.

I can actually hear the shocked intake of air as the reality of what I just said to Ben sinks in.

There's a lump forming in my throat, and I have to look down at the table.

"I mean, I was going to try. I didn't get very far, because what kind of person does that? What kind of person gets angry at someone for lying and cheating and all the things that you did to me back then, and then turns around and even considers doing the same things to you? Not the *same* things, obviously, but bad things. Things I stopped talking to my parents over."

I hear Ben's chair sliding across the wood floor before he stands up and walks over to my side of the table, taking the chair next to mine.

He puts his hand on my shoulder, and I shrug away from his touch so quickly, it's almost as if he's burned me.

"Don't," I say, my voice choked with emotion. "How can you even want to be near me?"

"Marisa-"

"I had lunch with Felicity today," I begin, and Ben sits back, pressing his lips together. "I took her aside, and asked her how Corinne was doing. This whole thing with my parents has been hard on her at school, and I know she's trying to protect me by keeping the worst of it to herself. Felicity went out there to visit her, and I just wanted to know how she was doing, you know? I thought Felicity would be comfortable telling me what Corinne isn't."

Ben's looking at me with sympathetic eyes. "What did she say?"

"That she was fine, because she had someone setting a good example for her." God, just replaying that conversation in my head makes my heart ache.

"You," Ben says quietly.

"Yeah." The tears are falling freely now, and when Ben slides his hand across my shoulders—back and forth—I take the comfort and don't flinch from it. "Honestly, I didn't know she looked up to me like that. I didn't think…I don't know, I didn't think I was the role model type."

"Of course you are."

"I heard that, and I thought, how can I let something terrible happen to her? How could I sit there and let someone follow through with that threat? I…" I swipe at my cheeks before I continue. "I just needed a distraction, so I went to see you. I was starting to have a panic attack, I think, or something kind of like it."

I pause for a moment, stopping to collect my thoughts. Ben has lied to me so many times in the past, but the guy I'm getting to know now…I don't think he'd ever do something like I did tonight. It's scary as hell to admit to him what I did, but it feels like the right thing to do. So, I take a deep breath.

"You were gone, and your secretary was gone, and your computer was just sitting there and I figured I had to try…" I'm a sobbing mess at this point, I don't even know if he can understand what I'm saying. I'm guessing he can't, because even after the beginning of my confession, he's still rubbing my back. Shouldn't he be getting as far away from me as possible? "So I sat at your desk, and I tried to guess your password, and what the fuck was I even doing, Ben?

"You come to me wanting to make a fresh start, and this is what I do?" He's still patiently rubbing my back, not backing away from me like he doesn't want anything to do with me ever again, just…being there for me. "I saw that picture you had of me on your desktop, and I felt sick because of what I was doing. I don't think I could ever tell you how sorry I am. There aren't words to even begin…"

Ben cups my face, letting his hand slide around to the back of my neck. He pulls me close, letting his forehead rest against mine, and for the first time since I walked into his office, I feel like I can *breathe* again.

"I forgive you," he says. Like it's easy as breathing. "I trust you."

"You shouldn't trust me."

I can feel the short huff of a laugh that he lets out against my collarbone, before he reluctantly pulls away.

"The very first reaction you had to what you were doing was to vomit in my trash can. That speaks worlds to me about the kind of person you are." He tucks my hair behind my ear. "As if I didn't know that already."

I can't think of anything to say that will correctly convey all the feelings I'm feeling about him right now, so I just lean in and kiss him softly.

He lets out a low, rumbling hum.

"When Felicity told me that Corinne looked up to me, I...I mean, even before she said that I would've done anything to protect her."

"Just like I'd do anything to protect Felicity."

I hadn't really thought about it like that. Of course he would've done the same thing for his sister, and that's probably why it's so easy for him to forgive what I tried to do for mine.

"I almost became like my parents. I...I can't let that happen.
"

He sighs, and the corners of his mouth quirk up. "You could never be like your parents. Not in a million years, no matter how many people try to blackmail you."

A rush of emotion that I'm incredibly hesitant to call love (even though it never really went away, even after our last breakup - but it's too soon for all that) warms me, and I lean in and kiss him again.

All that warmth cools a bit when Ben pulls away, and I see

the hesitant look in his eyes before he says, "There's something I need to ask you. I just...I have to know."

"What is it?" I ask, taking his hands in mine.

"When did this guy threaten you?"

"The other morning, after we had breakfast. He caught me as I was unlocking my door."

His shoulders slump in something that resembles relief. It takes me longer than it should to figure out why.

"Oh, Ben," I say, cradling his face in my hands. "No. Don't even think that."

If I had any doubt left in my mind that he was serious about the two of us this time around, it would've been dashed at the look in his eyes when he thought that the only reason I agreed to get back together with him was because I was being blackmailed.

"I just..."

"I know," I tell him. "I understand. But I decided to give this another go completely on my own. After this is over, whatever happens..."

"I'm not going to let anyone hurt Corinne," he says.

I want to believe him, and I know he'll do everything he can, but not even he can make a promise like that.

"Okay." I try to give him a reassuring smile. "When this is over, I'll still be around."

"Provided I don't fuck it up." He's being self-deprecating, and it's cute. It makes me stop thinking about the gravity of the situation for a minute or two.

I lean in and press my lips against his. "You're doing pretty well so far."

Ben and I have a few moments to ourselves before we have to put all of our personal issues aside and get to work on solving this incredibly huge problem that I've got. Unfortunately for me, the worst part of the conversation is coming, because security is on their way, and even though Ben knows more about what's going on than he did an hour ago, he still doesn't know anywhere close to everything.

Thankfully Ben decides not to ask me any questions until the security guys show up; that way I don't have to repeat myself.

It's a small blessing, but I'll take it.

Ben's head of security is a tall, broad, well-dressed man, who looks like he spends most of his day doing squats and lifting weights. He's bald and hard-looking, but incredibly nice. To me, at least. He's accompanied by a much smaller man who has a laptop computer cradled in his left arm.

Ben tells me their names, but I'm too keyed up to remember them.

They're both wearing suits, looking more like executives than the people who make sure those executives are safe.

They sit down across from Ben and me, and the shorter

one opens his laptop. Ben twines his fingers with mine as the questions start.

"Do you know the perpetrator?"

"No."

"Have you ever seen him before?" The smaller one asks as he types away on his laptop.

"Not that I'm aware of, no. He was wearing a hat and sunglasses. I couldn't really see his face."

"Are there surveillance cameras on your property?"

"Just one at the front door. His face isn't visible because of the cap, but I'll get the footage for you anyway."

The taller of the two of them nods.

"Is there anyone who could be targeting you or your sister?"

I shrug, trying to be lighthearted. "Only about half of Manhattan, and god knows who else my parents screwed over."

"We need to get a security team on the sister, stat," the taller guy says to the shorter one.

"I already have one," I say, and three pairs of eyes look at me, surprised. My purse is hanging from the back of the chair next to mine. I reach inside, and pull out a piece of paper, write the number of the point person from the security company on it, then slide it across the table.

"Where's the number for yours?" the taller security guard asks.

"My what?"

"Your security team, Marisa," Ben says, like I'm an idiot for not realizing this.

"I don't have one."

"Why the hell not?" he asks angrily. "How could you get one for Corinne but not for yourself?"

"I got one for Corinne right after my parents' arrest," I explain. "I didn't get that because of the pictures."

His eyes widen. "And still this managed to happen?" He looks over at the security team, and then back to me. "And why in the hell don't you have security?"

"I was scared to contact anyone after the guy approached me. I didn't want to do anything out of the ordinary."

"Like try to protect yourself!" he yells.

"He's got nude pictures of my sister that he could send out with the press of a button, Ben. Famous people can come back from that, but children of thieves embroiled in a national scandal don't. I was scared!"

Ben sets his elbows on the table, leans forward, and pinches the bridge of his nose. "How is that not the first fucking thing you did after the scandal went public?" he says lowly. And I can tell by the look on his face when he glances over at me that the other question he really wants to ask is how he didn't think of it before now.

"My lawyer told me I should, but-"

"But what? How was ensuring your own safety not at the top of your list?" he yells.

He's right, it was stupid. It was incredibly shortsighted and dumb of me to put my own ego above my safety. But I'm going to tell him the truth, even if it gob smacks him.

"I didn't want anyone to know I was scared. It seemed… weak."

I don't dare look at the security guys, who have surely heard idiotic things like that more than once. I do, however regret looking at Ben. His head is slumped down near the surface of the table, and he's rubbing at the back of his neck impatiently. A tell-tale sign that he's well on his way to losing it.

"Jesus Christ," he says, and I'm pretty sure I'm the only one who can hear it.

He takes a moment to get himself under control before he looks up at the larger security guy. "Take care of that."

The man nods.

"What if this guy sees one of them, and gets the idea that I've told someone about what happened?"

"To be honest, I don't give a fuck," Ben says, angry. "How could you be so careless with your own safety?"

"No," I say to the big guy. "I don't want anything out of the ordinary going on. He can't know!"

"Ma'am," the smaller guy says, sounding incredibly patient. "We're professionals, and if we do our job correctly - which we will, no one will be the wiser that you've got a detail on you. You have my word. I have a sister, I…I understand how terrible this must be for you. We won't let anything happen to either of you."

I pick at a growing hangnail on my left thumb, as I think about what he's telling me. I feel an immense amount of relief now that Ben knows what's going on. The nagging ache that I've felt in my chest, the inescapable worry about everything that was happening in my life is gone for the first time since all of this happened.

Hell, probably for the first time since my parents were arrested, if I'm being honest.

I really want to put all of this in someone else's hands. Let them spend all day and night trying to find this shitbag, and to let them figure out who he is and why he went through me to get something from Ben.

I want it so desperately.

Ben looks like he wants that, too. Like the entire balance of his world hinges on me telling these men that yes, I'll let them protect my sister and myself, and that I'll trust them enough to get this done right.

I want to.

God, I want to.

It's just difficult placing the fate of the person I love the most in this world in someone else's hands.

"Okay," I say, and I can actually feel the tension go out of Ben's shoulders.

He looks like he can finally breathe again.

"Does Corinne know about this?" he asks.

From the look on the security guys' faces, this was obviously going to be their next question.

"No," I say, plucking at that hangnail again, needing to focus my attention on something other than the questions at hand. "I was hoping I could take care of this without her knowing. I…" I shrug. "I wanted to protect her."

Ben reaches over, and cups the back of my head with his hand. He runs his fingers through my hair reassuringly, and he doesn't look angry anymore. Just sympathetic, like for the first time since all of this started, he understands where I'm coming from.

"Hiding it from her isn't protecting her," he says gently.

"I know," I say, feeling like I'm going to cry. I have to swallow past the painful lump in my throat. "I know that."

"You need to tell her, Miss Blake," tall security guy says. "We need information on the gentleman she was with that night. It might give us some clues as to who is behind this. If maybe he was part of it, too."

I nod. I need to give myself a few minutes to mentally prepare for that. "Okay."

"You're staying with me," Ben says. When I open my mouth to protest, he replies, "I'm not taking no for an answer."

Part of me wants to make it incredibly clear that he can't tell me what to do, that that's not how this thing between us is going to work. But I desperately need his help, and this is the first time in days that I've felt safe. I'd be foolish to walk away from that, and I don't want to be foolish anymore.

I want to get this taken care of and move on with my life.

"Okay," I reply.

"Now you know what you have to do," he says sympathetically.

Unfortunately, I do.

"Here," he says, offering me his hand. He helps me up, and leads me down a long hallway into his bedroom. The view from here is amazing; he doesn't even need to turn the lights on. The city lights coming through the floor-to-ceiling windows are all the light I need. The walls are brick, with no decoration. His bed is modern and neatly made, his watch and a few other things on his nightstand.

There's nothing on the nightstand on the opposite side of the bed, which is a strange thing to notice at a moment like this.

"Sit down," he says, motioning to the edge of the bed. "Make yourself comfortable. I'll be out in the dining room if you need me."

My heart skips a little at the thought of what I'm going to say to my sister, and part of me wants to ask him if he'll stay with me so I don't have to do it on my own. It would be nice to have a hand to hold onto when I deliver this news.

But, I've got to do it on my own.

Ben starts to walk away, but I tug on his hand, pulling him

back to me gently. He knows exactly what I'm looking for, and doesn't hesitate to lean down and press a soft kiss to my lips.

He whispers, "It's going to be okay. She's stronger than you think."

I nod, and watch him walk out the door.

I give myself a minute, then dial Corinne's number.

CHAPTER
Sixteen

A soft knock on the door pulls me out of my thoughts.

I'm still sitting on the edge of Ben's bed, with my cell phone cradled in my hands. I've been crying so much that my eyes are puffy and painful and throbbing. My cheeks are hot and covered with dried tears. I'm sure my makeup is a mess.

My head is pounding.

There's so much left to be done, but all I want to do is curl up in a ball and fall asleep until the world looks bright and new again, and everything in my body stops hurting.

Corinne took it pretty well, all things considered, but I suppose I shouldn't have expected anything less from my sister. She didn't react so positively to me telling her that I had actually planned on going through with the blackmailer's demand that I steal that program from Ben.

She was more upset by that than she was when I told her about the pictures the guy used to blackmail me with.

She cried and yelled, and asked me if I had learned anything at all from our parents, and reminded me that I didn't have any room to hate them if I became someone just like them.

That didn't feel very good.

She asked me to give her some time to think about things, and I told her that I would give her all the time that she needed. I let her know that Ben's security team was going to be in touch with her, and that they were going to send new guys to make sure she was safe.

She didn't fight me on it, so I knew this whole thing had her shaken up in a way that she didn't want to admit.

"Hey," Ben says as he pushes open the door. The light that is streaming in from the hallway strains my eyes, since they are already achy from all the crying. I squint, holding up a hand to block out the light. "Sorry." He takes a step inside the room, and shuts the door behind him.

He walks over to where I'm sitting, and hands me a cup of something warm.

"Hot chocolate. With the tiny marshmallows that I know you like."

I bring the cup up to take a whiff of the delicious smell, and let out a small moan.

The bed dips as Ben sits down next to me, and I blow on the hot liquid so I can take a sip.

"How did it go?" He places his hand on the small of my back, pressing his fingers into my skin. It's reassuring and warm; it makes me cuddle against his side for a little comfort.

"Not well. Not terrible, either."

"Is Corinne okay?" he asks, as his thumb slips underneath the hem of my shirt, and he rubs soothing circles against my skin.

"As okay as she can be. She's shaken up, but I think she'll be all right. She couldn't give me much information on the guy. They had met at a bar that night." She'd been reluctant to tell me that information, as if I of all people would judge her for having a one-night stand.

If only she knew all the terrible decisions I'd made in order to have sex. So, there's no judgment coming from me, just concern. Because if she's living in the kind of world where people are looking to fuck her for blackmailing purposes, then her life just got a whole lot more complicated, and probably a whole lot lonelier.

And that just makes me even angrier at my parents.

"The guys are going to call her now. They've got a team assembled, and they're going to send them over to meet her, and look in on this guy."

I look down, cradling my head in my hands. "She didn't know him, Ben. What if this guy sought her out as part of this plan? I don't want her living the kind of life where she has to be wary of every single guy who comes up to her in a bar."

"It's probably not a bad thing for her to be careful," he says, running his hand up and down my back.

"It's one thing to be careful, but it's another to have to worry that the guy is just having sex with you so that he can use pictures of it to blackmail your sister. That's a world I don't want her living in."

Ben sighs, and wraps me up in his arms. "That's a world she's living in now, regardless. And that isn't your fault, Marisa. That's your parents' fault."

"But we don't even know why this man chose me to go after you," I protest. "Maybe it is my fault."

Ben shakes his head, then lets out a long sigh. "You know I've always been a fixture in those goddamn tabloids. We were in them all the time when we were together-"

"And when we were breaking up," I add, because he's right. The two of us were fixtures in all those gossip rags back when we were dating. As the children of two high-profile families, our relationship was seen as a business merger as much as it was a romance by some people in the press.

"And when we were breaking up. Maybe this isn't about you or Corinne. Maybe it's about me. God knows I don't have a shortage of enemies in my field."

"Then why come to me?" I ask. That's the thing that I can't figure out in this mess. "We've only been seeing each other for less than a week, and Corinne told me she went home with that guy over a week ago. So this can't have anything to do with you and me, since we weren't even together when the pictures were taken."

"We only got back together a few days ago, but we've been seeing each other since before that," he reminds me.

"But who would even know about that?" I ask. "We were basically just fucking."

I can feel Ben's physical flinch as the words come out of my mouth. I don't like being so crass about it, but it's not like I'm not telling the truth. It was pretty much just physical between us until very recently.

"Unless," I say, remembering with startling clarity a detail I had forgotten until now: that car that I had seen parked down the street from the diner Ben and I ate at the morning I decided to give our relationship another shot. The car I was certain I saw a paparazzi sitting in.

What if it wasn't a paparazzi at all? What if someone had been watching me all this time?

"What?" Ben asks.

I take a deep breath, steeling myself for his reaction, because I know it's not going to be a good one. "The morning that we left the diner, I saw a car parked down the street. I thought maybe I saw a camera lens pointed at us, but I brushed it off."

Ben's head lolls back, as he looks up at the ceiling, exasperation written all over his gorgeous face. "Jesus, Marisa. Why didn't you say anything?!"

I'm quick to come to my own defense. "Because I'm no stranger to having my picture taken, Ben, especially with everything going on with my parents. I didn't really think anything of it at the time." I've brushed off photographers since the news of my scandal broke. I wonder how many times that's going to come back to bite me in the ass.

"Marisa," he sighs. I can tell he's doing his best to work through his frustration, because at this point, what's done is done. "You have to take your own safety seriously, okay? This…Christ, this isn't a joke. This isn't about your pride, do you understand that? You taking threats seriously, and taking your privacy seriously isn't admitting a weakness. It's showing that you're strong enough to do what it takes to keep yourself safe."

He's right, I know he is. I'm not even going to argue that. This insane need that I have to make sure people don't know how much things bother me is going to get me in some serious trouble one day. This is a wake-up call, and I've got to take it.

Ben turns toward me on the bed, takes my hands in his and presses kisses to my knuckles. "I know I hurt you," he says softly. "Repeatedly. And I'm sure that has something to do with the way that you try to hide that hurt, but please don't do that at the expense of your own safety. *Please*," he says, and I can tell that this has him rattled like nothing has before.

"I'm not going to fight you on the security detail," I assure him. "But this isn't about you, Ben." I give his fingers a squeeze.

"This isn't about you or what you did in the past. I've always been this way, always tried to hide my hurt from people. You were actually the only one I never did that with. When you hurt me, I let you know.

"My mother and father never looked kindly on weaknesses. When I was a kid and I skinned my knees, I never cried. When my nanny was the one who showed up to my ballet recitals, I never let my parents know how that made me feel. You," I say, reaching up and putting my hand on his cheek. "You were the only one I ever showed my real feelings to. If you hurt me, I wasn't afraid to show it."

That always baffled me about our relationship, honestly. Even though it was tumultuous for the most part, it was the most honest I've ever been with another person in my life.

"And I kept hurting you anyway," he says, his voice full of regret.

"I didn't say that to make you feel bad," I tell him. "I wanted you to know that I'm not this way because of anything you did. That I hid my hurt from everyone *but* you for the most part. So don't go taking on any blame that isn't yours to take, okay?"

I lean in and give him a reassuring kiss.

"Okay," he whispers against my lips. When he pulls away, he threads his fingers through mine. "I also thought you should know - I called Mia. She came over and picked up the thumb drive to see if she could find any traces that this jackass might've left behind on it."

"What, like fingerprints?" I ask stupidly.

The corner of Ben's mouth quirks up into a smile. "Digital fingerprints, yeah."

"You didn't want the security guys to do that?"

"She has more technical expertise. I trust her, and wanted to keep this in-house. And," he says, shifting a little, "she has some experience with this kind of stuff."

I scrunch my eyebrows together. "How? She just got out of college." Not trying to take a dig at her; I really like Mia. But from what she's told me, working with Ben is her first job out of school, and I don't want to take any chances with Corinne.

Ben doesn't seem all that bothered by my curiosity. "At some point, you two should sit down and get to know each other. You both have a protective streak a mile wide, and you would appreciate that about each other."

I'm still kind of confused about where he's going with this. "She was blackmailed in order to keep nude pictures of her sister from being released world-wide?"

I'm teasing him, but only a little. There's a lot of curiosity in there, too.

"No," he says with a small huff of a laugh. "But it's not my story to tell, or my place to tell you. She just knows what it's like to go to some pretty extreme lengths to protect someone she cares about. She's a lot like you that way."

He says that last line with so much affection that I have to lean in and kiss him again.

"Is everyone gone?" I ask.

"Yeah," he says, nodding. "I think we've done everything we can for tonight. Hopefully tomorrow we'll have some answers." He reaches up and slides the pads of his thumbs along the circles beneath my eyes. "You look tired. You should get some sleep."

"I'll try," I tell him. Even though I've made some pretty big strides tonight, I'm still not feeling all that confident in our chances. I mean, I feel better about them than I did before, but still not all that great. Still, I don't doubt that everything that's happened will keep me awake.

"You're safe here with me. You know that, right?"

I nod. "Yeah, I know."

"And I'll be right in the other room, okay? Just yell for me, and I'll come running."

What I consider telling him is that I don't want him in the other room. I want him here with me. I know that I drew a pretty firm line in the sand when I told him that I wanted to give this another go.

I told him sex was off the table, so I could keep my head around him in the early stages of whatever this is between us. But tonight, I just want him to hold me in his arms, to cradle my head against his chest. I want to feel the warmth of his lips on my skin, and the weight of his body on mine.

I want to feel a connection with him.

"I'll go get you an old t-shirt to sleep in," he says, as he stands.

136

I can't help but smile, knowing that he remembers that I like to sleep in his clothes, when I sleep in anything at all around him.

Before he can get too far, I reach out and give his hand a gentle tug. "Don't go."

He turns and looks at me, eyebrow raised, a hopeful look on his face that he's trying like hell to hide. I know that he's trying to do everything right this go 'round, that he's willing to go without sex for as long as I want to wait.

But he wants me, I can see it in his eyes. "What?"

And I want him, too. "Don't go," I repeat. "Stay with me tonight."

That hopeful look in his eyes grows, but he gives me another out anyway. "Are you sure?"

"I'm sure," I reply, pulling him down to the bed. And the strange thing is that knowing he'll leave if I want him to—no questions asked—makes me want him to stay even more.

After he leans down and kisses me, he says, "Did you forget the rules?"

"I don't care about the rules anymore. And I'm pretty sure I won't be needing an old t-shirt to sleep in."

There's a low rumble in his chest, something that sounds almost like a growl. I stand up and wrap my arms around his neck so I can kiss him again, then turn his body, and press on his shoulders, letting him know that I want him to sit down on the edge of the bed.

When Ben and I first started dating, and everything was new and wonderful, I took for granted that it would always feel that way. Now, I know that things aren't always good, and I won't always feel the way that I feel right now, like there's something to be hopeful for and thankful for, and it's all because of him.

I want him to feel what I'm feeling, so I plant my knees on the bed, on either side of his legs, and grind myself on him, where he's already hard for me.

He lets out a soft moan before he presses his lips to mine, his fingertips trailing along the waistband of my pants and slipping below, his roughened thumbs brushing against my sensitive skin.

We kiss, dirty and desperate, all teeth and tongue.

Somehow I manage to pull myself away from him, only long enough to slip off my shirt, and then unclasp my bra. Ben looks up at me with some expression that I've never seen from him before, full of wonder and love and a thousand other beautiful, fleeting things.

He's seen me naked a thousand times, but this is the first time he's ever looked at me like *this*.

Ben slides his hand up, across my belly, and brings it to rest over my rapidly beating heart. He holds it there for a moment or two, then reaches over and cups my breast as he presses a kiss against my sternum.

He kisses a trail along the path he makes with his hand,

then circles my nipple with his tongue, pulling it between his teeth as I grip his hair between my fingers.

My head lolls back as I get lost in sensation, his teeth, tongue, and lips working magic, and his stubble scraping across skin that grows more sensitive by the second. I'm rocking against his lap, and Ben thrusts up, moaning as he gets a little friction.

He grips my ass and moves my body against his, his eyes fluttering shut as he works himself up. I need something a little more intimate than this; I want skin on skin in any way I can get it, so I climb off of his lap, ignoring the sounds of protest he makes.

They disappear when I drop to my knees, and Ben catches on to what it is I'm about to do.

I undo his belt buckle, then unbutton his pants. I cup him through the fabric just to tease him before I slowly slide his zipper down and reach into his boxer briefs to free his erection.

I lean forward and lick a stripe from the base of his cock to the tip, never breaking eye contact with Ben. His body goes slack as I take him in my mouth, and he props his right arm behind him to hold his weight as he threads his left hand through my hair to guide my mouth.

I take him in as far as I can, licking and sucking the way I know he likes. He's feeling good, relaxed and tense at the same time; I can tell by the way his eyelids flutter closed and his breathing picks up. He's thrusting up a little into my mouth, even though I can tell he's trying to keep what little bit of control he can.

"Feel so good," he manages, as I take his balls in my hand and give them a gentle tug. He lets out a long, tortured groan, and pulls me up, kissing me roughly.

In a move that's so quick I barely even register what happens, Ben flips me over, so I'm lying on the mattress. He's holding himself above me, and all I want to do is turn my head and lick the straining muscles in his bicep.

Ben's belt buckle is grazing my stomach, giving me chills, and his eyes are dark and mischievous. He moves down my body, sliding my pants off, not even bothering with my panties. He just settles down between my legs, uses his big, rough hands to spread them wide.

Ben moves my underwear to the side, and he doesn't tease me. He just puts his mouth exactly where I want it. He licks and sucks, paying special attention to my clit, as his left hand finds my nipple.

I moan, and grind down on his face a little. That simple movement must really get him going if the enthusiasm with which he continues getting me off is any indication.

"You taste so good," he says, his voice making me vibrate in all the right places. I shift my hips to help him get a better angle, and he gets so frustrated with the presence of my undies that he rips them clean off.

He's never done something like that before, and honestly,

watching it happen ticked my arousal up about another ten notches. I grip his hair tightly, using it for leverage, and I buck my hips against him, chasing my impending release.

I come in seconds, white-hot pleasure radiating out into my toes and my fingertips. Ben keeps his mouth on me, working me down, kissing the insides of my thighs, and rubbing my hips with his talented hands.

"C'mere," I say, crooking my finger.

He responds immediately, pressing his body against mine as he crawls up my body for a kiss.

When I feel the tip of his cock against me, I very nearly push down, just wanting to keep feeling this connection with him. I'm desperate for it at this point, despite the fact that I'm still feeling the ripples from my first orgasm.

I know that's what he wants too, because he rocks his hips against mine. He's probably not even thinking clearly right now, his common sense completely lost in a haze of lust. I have to be the one to look out for both of us now.

"Condom," I say, my voice all raspy and low.

"What?" He pulls back, almost adorably confused. It's always been a little difficult for Ben to shake the haze of lust once he lets it take hold of him.

"We need a condom, Ben."

His eyes widen, and he almost manages to hide the surprise that he had gotten so far without putting one on yet. He reaches over to his nightstand and opens the drawer.

There was a time when I would've let him fuck me without any protection, but I'm smarter than that now

One pregnancy scare with him was one too many.

"Sorry," he says as he rolls on the condom. "I got a little distracted."

He leans down and gives me a sweet kiss, planting his elbows on the bed for leverage as he twines our fingers together. He latches onto my neck as he slides into me. We're both so far gone and desperate for each other that we frantically rock into each other.

We kiss, and I wrap my legs around Ben, needing him as close as I can get him, let him push me higher and higher, as I turn my head and breathe in the smell of him, all sweaty and soapy and perfect.

My second orgasm isn't as strong as my first, but it's enough to get lost in, enough to make me feel like I'm light as air. It's enough to pull Ben along after me, and his body stiffens as he loses his rhythm, pressing his forehead into the crook of my neck and chanting my name as he comes.

We lie together, holding each other, for a few minutes, until Ben starts softening inside of me. We both groan when he pulls himself up to discard the condom, and I miss the warmth of his body immediately. It doesn't take him long to clean up, and when he climbs back into bed, he wraps his body around mine.

As usual, he's the big spoon to my little.

"That was amazing," he says, nuzzling into my hair. "You're amazing."

"It was amazing," I reply, squeezing his bicep.

"Thanks for the orgasms," I tease.

Ben laughs, and it's warm against the still-drying sweat on the back of my neck. "My pleasure. Literally."

I can practically feel Ben's smile. I know he sounds content.

And despite everything that's going on in my life and all the ways it could go wrong, I am, too.

CHAPTER
Seventeen

Ben and I are both so exhausted by everything that happened the night before, we sleep in a little the following morning. It's a work day for both of us; I have a few conference calls with potential advertisers, and Ben has two meetings that he has to be in the office for.

I make a couple of omelettes out of what little I can find in Ben's fridge, and the two of us eat side-by-side as we lay out our non-work plans for the day, all of which involve dealing with the Corinne crisis on our hands.

Mia set up some kind of an algorithm that would send her an alert if the scumbag who was blackmailing me tried to sell any of Corinne's pictures. Apparently it would let her know if he even made contact with someone and let them know that he had such a thing. The logistics of that were beyond me, even though Ben patiently explains it to me at least three times.

Knowing that we have an extra layer of security thanks to Mia's skills adds a layer of calm to my still frazzled nerves. We're taking care of things, but we're not taking care of them quickly enough for my tastes. I know that we have to be a little patient and take our time to make sure that everything goes smoothly, since one wrong move could trigger mass distribution of those pictures, but I'd rather this be over with sooner rather than later.

For her part, Corinne said that if the pictures got out, she'd handle it. Obviously, she'd rather that very private part of her life not be released for public consumption, but she's a resilient young woman. She'll bounce back from this if she has to.

Still, I'm going to do everything I can to make sure that she doesn't have to.

The head of Ben's security team—the taller guy from last night, whose name I now know is Stuart—stops by before Ben leaves for the office.

Stuart tells me that I need to go home for a little while today, at least a couple of hours, just in case that psycho blackmailer is actually watching me like he says he is. Stuart doesn't want me off the grid for too long; he thinks that the more I can keep up with my daily routine, the better.

His idea is this: He'll head over to my neighborhood for a good surveillance spot now. Ben's driver will drop me off in front of my place, before driving Ben to his office. It'll look to the outside like the sleepover it was. I'll make my morning coffee run like I usually do, and Stuart will have a guy on me. I'll go home and work for a few hours like normal, and then Ben can pick me up on his way back from the office.

"Someone will have eyes on you at all times," Stuart assures me. I probably look worried out of my mind, which isn't too far from the truth. "As an extra precautionary measure, you'll have this." He takes my hand, and presses a small black fob into my palm.

"What is it?" I ask.

"A panic button. We're going to be nearby, but we won't be in the house with you. If something happens, and I mean *if*, then I want you to press this red key. We'll come for you right away."

"Okay," I say, carefully pocketing the fob.

"I trust your judgment," Stuart continues. "Please only use this if you absolutely have to. If you're feeling spooked, I've added my cell number to the contact list on your phone. I'll have that on me at all times. Send me a text if you think there's something that I need to check out. We don't want to alert anyone who might be watching that anything is out of the ordinary."

I completely understand that. It's been one of my worries. "If something is scary but not immediately dangerous, I'll text you."

Stuart nods. "I'll have my phone on me at all times."

Ben gently puts his hand on mine. "Promise me you'll use that."

I look at him curiously. "Of course I will."

"You were so reluctant to ask for help because you were worried that this guy would realize that something was out of the ordinary; I just wanted to make sure that if push comes to shove you'll get the help you need, regardless."

Ben actually looks a little terrified at the prospect that I might be too concerned about appearances to ask for help when I need it. Given the fact that it took me being on the verge of a nervous breakdown in his office to ask for help with this situation in the first place, I can't say that I blame him.

I press my hand against his cheek, then give him a short, chaste kiss. "I promise. I'll press this button if I think I'm in immediate danger."

Ben rests his forehead against mine. "Okay."

"I'm going to head out," Stuart says, interrupting the moment. "I'll let your driver know when he's clear to leave. Any questions?"

I shake my head.

Ben says, "No."

Stuart walks out the front door, and Ben turns to me.

"I don't like the idea of you going home alone."

I knew this was coming, and honestly, it's endearing. "I'm just going to do some work there. Me spending the night here with you isn't out of the ordinary, but me not coming home for days is. I'll do some work, keep up appearances, and then we'll meet somewhere for dinner."

"I'll pick you up for dinner," he says, looking a little more relaxed than he did a minute ago. "I've still got some wooing to do."

I can't help but smile. "I'm glad the wooing is still on, considering I broke my other rule."

"Wooing you is my pleasure," he says, leaning in for a kiss with a breathtaking smile on his face.

"And breaking my rule was my pleasure."

He hums against my lips. "And mine."

"Many times," I say, giggling.

"Maybe tonight we can break some more rules." His hand trails up the inside of my thigh, over the fabric of the pants that I wore here yesterday.

"We broke the rules three times last night," I remind him.

"Tonight, let's try for four."

I'm looking forward to that. "After dinner."

"And wooing."

"Mmm-hmm," I reply, giving him another kiss.

It's nice to get lost in possibility right now. To make plans that completely leave our current situation out of the equation. Because the fact of the matter is that our world at dinner time might look a lot different than it does right now. We might be dealing with yet another crisis. Or, hopefully, we'll be putting this one to bed.

Either way, the planning is a nice distraction.

Ben's cell phone beeps, and he pulls it out of the breast

pocket of his suit.

"Time to go," he says, helping me up from my chair.

As he walks over to the table by the door, collecting his laptop bag. I take a moment to admire the view: Ben's in the kind of business where he doesn't dress up very frequently. He's always dressed *nicely*, but suits aren't part of his wardrobe on a daily basis.

It's a damn shame, too, because suits look sinful on this man. The one he's wearing today is steel grey, paired with a crisp white shirt and a blue silk tie that really sets off his gorgeous eyes.

"What?" he asks, a smile spreading across his lips.

"That's a good suit," I say, walking over to him. "You should wear it more often."

He practically preens under my compliment, and it takes my mind off of what I'm about to do: go home and pretend like absolutely nothing is wrong.

"C'mon," he says, taking my hand.

I let him lead me out the door and down to the car. During our ride, he holds my hand, and I sit in silence thinking about how far I've come since yesterday.

Corinne has new people looking out for her, ones that will be observant enough to look out for someone trying to seduce her into a compromising position. She's going to get acquainted with them this morning.

Mia has an eye out for someone trying to sell those

pictures, which is a relief in and of itself.

Ben hooked me up with security that makes me feel truly protected, like they've taken my concerns to heart and are going to make sure that everything is okay.

I have a number to text if I feel uncomfortable, and a panic button to sound off if I think I'm in danger.

Still, I can't help the feeling of dread that nags at me when Ben drops me off. He kisses me, lingering a little, like he feels it, too.

The day passes mostly without incident, and I manage to get through quite a lot of work before Ben's due to pick me up for dinner.

I'm ready and waiting for him at 7, and don't think much of him running late. That's pretty typical for him. By 7:45, when my texts and calls have gone unanswered, my phone lights up.

It's Stuart.

"Hello?" I say, trying to sound like I'm in control, and not dangerously close to spiraling.

"Don't panic," Stuart says, which does absolutely nothing to keep me calm. "I'm sending a car for you."

"What happened?"

"It's Ben."

CHAPTER
Eighteen

I n an emergency room cubicle that takes us entirely too long to get to, Ben sits with his legs dangling off the bed, his head bowed, his injured hand cradled against his chest.

I rush into the room like an hysterical maniac, having pushed past a number of nurses in order to get to him. No one told me how bad it was, just that he was "going to be okay."

I spent most of the ride over here thinking that maybe he'd be in a coma, or shot, or that he'd been hit by a car. I had no idea what to expect. But when I see his hangdog expression as I walk into the room, that he's upright and conscious, I'm glad that at least the worst of my fears have been put to rest.

He's fine, he's moving under his own power, and there aren't any wires coming out of his arm or any machines hooked up to his chest.

This is good, a best-case scenario.

I can work with this.

I walk over to him, and crook my fingers beneath his chin, tilting his head up so he has to look at me. He has a split lip, and his left hand looks terrible, all bleeding and bruised and swollen.

I give him a soft kiss, but he pulls away from it too soon. He doesn't meet my eyes.

"Are you okay?" I ask. I have no idea what happened or why he's here, but I have to know the answer to that question first.

He nods. "It's over."

"What?" I ask, not entirely sure that I heard him correctly. "What's over?"

Stuart steps up behind me, holding a picture in his hands. My heart stops when I see it. It's the man whose identity I've been trying to find ever since he showed up on my front step with that envelope full of pictures so many days ago.

"Does this guy look familiar?" Stuart asks.

I nod, speechless. It's too good to be true. It's too much to think that just like that, with a phone call and what looks like a broken hand, that this could all be over.

"Preston Pollard," Stuart says. "That's his name. We got him, and our guys in California nabbed his associate, the guy who conned your sister."

"And the pictures?"

"We've deleted every trace of them," Stuart assures me.

"How can you be sure?"

"Under the threat of injury and severe financial penalties, we got Mister Pollard to hand over all copies. If there are more and he didn't disclose that to us, trust me. He'll pay," Stuart explains.

I guess this is as sure a thing as I'm going to get in this day and age.

"Does Corinne know? Did someone call her?"

Stuart nods. "She knows, although I expect she'd like to hear from you later. She knows we were bringing you in."

"What happened, exactly?" I ask, sliding my hand along the smooth ridges of Ben's tense shoulders. "Is this related? What happened to you?"

It's a rapid fire of questions, but I've just been given so much information that it's difficult to focus on just one thing.

"Slow down," Stuart says, with a small smile that you can only give someone when you know everything is going to be okay.

"Okay, let's start with this: Is your hand okay? How did that happen?"

"My hand's fine," Ben says absently, still looking at the floor.

"It's broken." Stuart looks at Ben. "They're going to come and set it soon."

"How did that happen?" I ask again. I'm guessing the answer is something that both of them know I won't want to hear.

"I beat the shit out of that guy," Ben says. He doesn't sound proud of it though, just ashamed.

"Can someone please fill me in on what happened, exactly? Was he after me, or Ben? Or Corinne?"

Stuart scrubs his hand over his face. "All three of you, actually."

For whatever reason, that wasn't an answer I was prepared to hear. "Why?"

"He was an employee of mine," Ben says. "He was working on the project he wanted you to steal the schematics for."

"He wasn't doing a very good job," Stuart adds.

"I'm a pretty good judge of character. We hire the best talent from the best schools. Sometimes I make a mistake."

I'm not really sure what to say to that, so I continue rubbing Ben's shoulders, hoping to work out some of the stubborn tension that doesn't want to come out.

"So, you fired him?" I ask. It doesn't take a genius to put that puzzle together.

Ben nods. "A few weeks ago. He started missing work, not calling in. His manager counseled him about it a few times, but he started getting agitated. Turns out he was having some personal problems."

"What kind of personal problems?" I ask. Breakups can make a person act irrationally. So can money- "Oh." It hits me like a ton of bricks, right in the center of my chest.

"Mister Pollard had a trust fund, and he took a meeting with your father a month and a half ago," Stuart explains.

That's all he needs to say.

"Why go after Corinne, though? I asked him if he wanted money, and he told me he didn't."

"He was angry and desperate, Marisa," says Stuart. "He got overambitious, wanting to embarrass your sister, tie you into knots, and get his hands on the real cash cow in Ben's program."

"He promised this guy in California a cut?" I ask.

Stuart nods. "Something like that."

"I still don't understand how we wound up in the hospital, though."

Stuart gives Ben a long look, like he's giving him the chance to explain himself. Ben's focus stays on the floor.

"Mia found a digital signature on the thumb drive Mister Preston gave you that let us know who he was. Ben insisted on coming along when we went to question him. I'll let him tell you the rest," Stuart says.

The nurse enters the room at the most inopportune moment, and Stuart excuses himself to go make some phone calls. Apparently he's got some unfinished business with the police, who have Preston Pollard locked up, charges pending.

"Time to get a cast on that," she says, way too cheery for the situation at hand.

"Do you want me to stay?" I ask Ben, desperate to get

through to him somehow, to break him out of this funk he's in. I want to know his side of the story, how he went from a ride-along with Stuart to being on the receiving end of a cast.

He shakes his head. "No. Go call Corinne."

"Ben," I plead, crouching down so I can look him in the eye.

He takes my hand in his good one, and gives it a squeeze before bringing it up to his mouth, where he presses a kiss to my knuckles.

"Go, I'll be fine. I'll see you when I'm done."

The nurse gives me a soft, understanding smile. "If you take a seat in the waiting room, I'll come out and get you when he's all finished."

I'm reluctant to leave, but that's clearly what Ben wants.

I nod, and head out of the door.

CHAPTER
Nineteen

"Hey," I say, standing on the small courtyard right off of the waiting room in the emergency wing of this hospital.

I can actually hear the smile in Corinne's voice. "Hey."

"How are you?" I ask. "Relieved, I hope?"

"Relieved, grateful, in awe. So thankful to you, Marisa. You have no idea."

I can't help but grin. "You should be thankful to Ben," I tell her. "He's the one who got the ball rolling on all of this once I told him."

"I'm sorry I yelled at you the other night. I didn't mean what I said, about you becoming like Mom and Dad."

"Don't apologize," I explain. "You didn't say anything that wasn't true, Corinne."

"I was angry and scared, and I lashed out. I appreciate that you want to make me feel better about it, but that doesn't mean that I'm any less sorry."

"I appreciate your apology," I say, brushing a strand of hair back behind my ear. "But, it was you who made me realize that I needed to ask for help."

"What do you mean?"

"I was worried about you. I always worry about you, but now with things the way they are with our family, I…sometimes I get a little nervous that you're not being completely honest with me about how things are for you. I don't want you to be angry about this, but I had lunch with Felicity the other day, and I asked about you."

I hear Corinne sigh on the other end of the line. "I know."

"You…what?"

Corinne laughs. "I know. Felicity told me."

"Oh," I reply, not sure how else to respond.

"She was right, you know."

"About what?"

"I look up to you, Marisa. When you told me what you planned to do to Ben, I was disappointed. But that feeling wasn't even in the same vicinity of how proud of you I was when you told me you reached out for help. Or how grateful I feel to you and Ben right now."

The tears are falling down my cheeks before I even register them, and I honestly can't believe that I lucked out with such an amazing sister.

"You have no idea how nice it is to hear that," I admit. I'm not even trying to hide the fact that I'm crying.

I hear the sniffle on the other side of the line, and I know that Corinne is crying, too. "Thank you so much, Marisa. For everything that you do for me, that you've done for me. These past few months could've been so miserable, but they haven't been. And that's because of you."

"I'd do anything for you, Cor."

"I know," she whispers.

"We have to stick together. You and me. Always."

"Always," she replies. "Is Ben there? Can I talk to him?"

"He's…uh, we're at the hospital right now."

"Is he okay?" she asks, an edge of panic in her voice.

"Yeah, just a broken hand."

"So, he beat the shit out of the guy, huh?"

"I'm not actually sure what happened," I admit. "He doesn't seem to be too anxious to talk about it."

"Give him some time," she tells me. "And take good care of him."

I smile. "I will. Oh, and just so you know…"

"Hmm?"

"That security detail is sticking around until this thing with Mom and Dad dies down, okay?"

"I won't fight you on mine as long as you don't try to get rid of yours," she replies mischievously.

"I'm not going to get rid of mine."

"Good. I don't want to worry about you."

"I think I worry enough for the both of us," I tell her.

"Maybe you should take a break on that for a while. Spend some time with your boyfriend, and get to know each other again. Have faith that your sister is out here in the sunshine having a grand old time."

"That doesn't do much to stop the worrying," I tease.

Corinne laughs, and it's a wonderful sound. "I love you, Marisa."

I smile. "I love you, too."

CHAPTER
Twenty

After an uncomfortable ride in complete silence, Ben's driver drops us off at his apartment. He's a little bit groggy from the pain pills the nurse gave him before he was discharged from the hospital, but he's walking under his own power. Still, I slide my arm around his waist to help keep him steady.

I'm spending the night here at his place, while Stuart and his team comb my brownstone for any sort of surveillance that Preston Pollard might have set up there.

They did a quick sweep earlier and didn't find anything, but everyone would feel better with a thorough once-over. Besides, I don't want to leave Ben alone tonight.

He's definitely hurting physically, but there's something nagging at him that he won't share with me. I don't want to pressure him to speak up about it, but honestly I'm getting a little frustrated with his standoffishness. If he needs space for whatever reason, then I'll give it to him. But he's not asking me to stay away, and he's not letting me get close, either.

I ask him if he'd like me to help him get into a pair of sweats he can sleep in, but he prefers doing it himself, refusing even the little bit of assistance I try to give him when he's having difficulty shrugging out of his shirt.

Confident that he's okay on his own, I go out into the kitchen, and pull the prescription that we got filled at a pharmacy on our way home out of my bag. Ben insisted that he didn't want any pain pills, and actually got angry with me when I so much as suggested that he didn't need to get all manly about it, but I figure it's good to have them at the ready anyway.

I've never broken anything, but I know it can't feel very good, and sleeping is going to be a challenge.

I take a glass out of the cupboard and fill it with water, wanting Ben to have something ready to drink if he's thirsty, or wakes up needing a pill.

I wrack my brain thinking of anything else I can get for him that will make him more comfortable or more likely to sleep, but my mind is a blank. Even though I'm not the one who spent most of the night in the hospital getting the bones in my arm put back together, I'm still exhausted.

It's mental taxation from the past few days. I still can't believe this is over. Well, the threatening part of it, at least.

Ben's still dealing with something that I wish he'd share so I could help him through it.

Maybe I should just let it go for tonight. He needs to rest, and he's not going to do that if I'm nagging him. Tomorrow, if he's still shutting me out, we'll have a talk.

I'll give him tonight.

With the glass of water and bottle of pills in hand, I walk back to the bedroom. Ben is sitting on the edge of the bed, looking out the window. The moonlight shines across his body, illuminating his nearly perfect profile. Even now, after a day like today, I'm caught off guard by how beautiful he is.

I never could deny how good he looked on the outside, but it seems like the time that we spent apart these past five years have helped develop that goodness inside, too.

I want to know more about that man.

He's been so supportive and amazing the past few days, that all I want to do is walk over, set down the water, and wrap myself around him. I want to beg him to talk to me.

But I don't.

I walk over to where he's sitting, and put down the glass of water and the painkillers.

"In case you need them," I say. I planned on setting them down and then going into the living room, because it doesn't seem like he wants any company tonight, but I can't leave without touching him.

My fingertips slide across the stubble on his cheek, and he

closes his eyes and leans into my hand.

I lean down and kiss his forehead. "I'll be in the other room if you need me."

His eyes dart up, looking almost panicked. "Don't go," he says, his voice completely wrecked.

"Are you sure?" I ask.

He nods. "Yes. Stay."

I don't need to be convinced.

I pull back the covers, and help Ben slide under them, then he pulls me in close. I wrap my body around his, careful of his injured arm, and lay my head on his chest.

With the steady beating of his heart beneath my cheek, it doesn't take long for me to drift off to sleep.

In the very early hours of the morning, I wake up to an empty bed, and cold sheets where Ben was lying just hours before, when we fell asleep together. The glass of water is still sitting on the nightstand untouched.

The bathroom light isn't on, either.

Even though I promised myself I would give him his space, there's a loud, niggling voice in my brain that keeps telling me to go to him. To find him and talk this out, because there's clearly something bothering him that time isn't going to fix.

I roll over to the edge of the bed, and let my feet dangle. I'm in nothing but one of Ben's old t-shirts, and my feet are cold, so I slide them into the slippers that he keeps on his side of the bed.

Stifling a yawn, I run my fingers through my hair as I trudge out of the bedroom and into the living room. I thought maybe I'd find him watching an old movie—something he used to do when he couldn't sleep—but the TV isn't on, and the rest of the apartment is dark and quiet.

I start to feel a little panicked, my mind wandering into worst-case scenario territory, when I see that the door to his balcony is open.

Ben is sitting there, bathed in moonlight, feet up on the railing, lost in thought.

I walk over to the balcony door, then knock lightly a few times, not wanting to startle him.

He looks over, and gives me a tight smile.

"Couldn't sleep?" I ask.

He shakes his head. "No."

"Do you want me to get your pills?"

He turns his head, and gives me a look that I can't quite read. It's almost like he's trying to talk himself into sharing whatever's bothering him with me. I don't want to pressure him into doing anything he's not ready for, so I stand there and wait for him to come to whatever conclusion he's trying to get to.

"This isn't something that a pill can fix," he says, finally, *finally* giving me an answer. Something I can work with to pull him out of this funk.

"What can fix it?" I ask. "A hug? I've got plenty of those. I'm also a pretty good listener, or so I've been told."

"C'mere," he says, lowering his feet from the railing. He scoots over in the chair, which is too big for one person, but not quite big enough for two. When I step in front of him, he wraps his good arm around my waist, and pulls me down until I'm sitting mostly on the chair, with my legs slung over his thighs.

"You ready to tell me what's going on?" I ask. I reach up and slide my fingertips along the curve of his jaw, something I know that he likes, and has comforted him before.

He closes his eyes, lets out a deep breath, and I can feel his muscles relax just a little.

"I lost it tonight," he says, looking down at his cast.

"Wanna tell me why?" I reach up and run my fingers through his hair. His eyes flutter closed for a second, as he figures out what he's going to say next.

"It all happened so fast. I was so angry at this guy for threatening you, for threatening Corinne...I wanted to *see* him. I wanted to have the chance to talk to him.

"One of Stuart's guys was holding him in a room in my building, waiting for the police to come. The way he talked about Corinne, about you..." Ben shakes his head, as if he's trying to get rid of the memories. "Like you were things, not even people. He said something filthy about Corinne; honestly,

I can't even remember what it was, and I just…snapped."

He looks so guilt-ridden and awful that I'm not sure what the right thing to say here is. That it was okay for him to do it? Obviously he doesn't think so. It's a wonder that he isn't in jail for that himself. Do I chastise him? He seems to be doing enough of that on his own.

Instead I just lean in and press a tender kiss against his temple.

"We've had a stressful few days, Ben."

He shrugs off that statement, ignoring it completely.

"The worst thing about it, aside from everything the guy had done…listening to him talk about you two the way he did, like you were expendable, it…it reminded me of myself a little bit."

"What?" I ask, surprised. "Ben, no." Even on his shittiest, most awful day, Ben would never have conned a woman into bed to do what these men did to Corinne. Not ever.

"Yes. It made me think about all the times I fucked around on you with women who didn't mean anything to me…seeing that in someone else, it…flipped a switch in me."

"Ben," I say hesitantly. "This guy…he paid someone to trick Corinne into bed. He used her as a means to an end. No matter what you did in the past, no matter how awful it made me feel…you never did that."

His gaze finally meets mine, and I can actually see the pain in his eyes.

"Yes, I did. My actions weren't the same, but the intention behind them was. I used those women to distract myself from how scared I was of being with you. It was a means to an end."

I close my eyes and shake my head, trying to figure out how I can get him to understand what I'm telling him. I don't want him seeing any part of himself in a guy like Preston Pollard.

"Did you misrepresent yourself to any of those women? Did they think they were getting anything more from you than sex?"

He shakes his head. "No."

"Did you trick any of them into bed?"

He shakes his head. "No."

Good. This is a start. "Ben, you were a terrible boyfriend, I'm not going to deny that. And you did shitty things and treated people terribly, but you're not a criminal. You were a careless, insecure, immature guy back then. But you're trying to be better. You learned from your mistakes, and that's what matters."

He looks up at me like he so desperately wants to believe what I'm telling him. I'm not sure that I have any other words I can use to convince him, so I press a kiss against his lips, hoping that will do a little to drive the point home.

"Will you tell me something?"

"Anything," I reply.

"Our last breakup," he begins, and every muscle in my

body tenses up instantaneously. "What finally did it?"

"You mean apart from all the cheating?" I'm trying to deflect, trying to figure out what answer I'm going to give to the question I'm sure he's going to ask me.

"Yeah. That time seemed different than the others."

"That time *was* different than the others," I admit. "You really want to work all of this out right now?"

Ben takes a deep breath, and lets out it on a slow exhale. "Yes. We have to talk about it sometime, right? Much as I'd like to pretend like I hadn't been so terrible to you, I think we need to talk about it if we're ever going to be able to move on."

I can't deny that he's right about that. Even though we both decided to give our relationship another shot, there is still some unfinished business between us. We're going to drag that baggage around with us until we either deal with it, or it becomes too heavy to carry anymore.

"If you're sure," I say. I don't know if I'm hoping he'll take the out for his sake, or for mine.

Ben just gives me a bashful smile. "I'm sure."

I close my eyes, and take a deep breath, trying to work up the nerve to say what I need to say. I've been holding onto it for a long time, and it's only right that I tell him. I should've told him this a long time ago.

Even though it's tempting to look away, to make sure I can't see the hurt in his eyes when I say what I'm about to say, I keep my eyes focused on his.

"Marisa," he says, his voice pleading. Maybe he thinks I'm going to stall or refuse. I'm just trying to gather up my strength for this.

"I was pregnant," I tell him.

His eyes go wide, and I know he stops breathing for a second. I decide to keep talking instead of giving him a minute to let it all sink in.

"You were supposed to meet me for dinner at my apartment one night," I recount, wondering if he has any recollection of this at all. "My period was two weeks late, and I was terrified. I had been trying to figure out a way to bring it up to you for days, but it never seemed like the right time."

I reach down and play with the hem of Ben's shirt that I'm wearing, because his steady gaze is too much for me to take. I can actually *feel* the weight of his eyes on me, and I can't let myself break down now.

"I had worked up the courage to do it that night, and I had bought every test known to man. I waited and waited, but you never showed. You weren't answering my calls. So, I went ahead and took the tests. Every single one of them was positive."

"Jesus, Marisa," he whispers, his voice completely broken. There are tears in his eyes, and I just can't let myself absorb all that right now.

"I was crying my eyes out, and I wanted to see you. I went over to your apartment, and knocked on the door. Oliver answered. He told me he hadn't seen you, but thought you'd be home soon. I decided to wait for you in that park on the corner, you remember the one?"

He nods, but it's almost robotic. Maybe he knows what's coming, or maybe he's nervous because he doesn't.

"I walked to the park, and there was a couple there. Kissing, laughing. The guy had her pressed up against the ladder to the monkey bars."

Ben gently slides my legs off of his lap, and stands, gripping the railing with his good hand.

"It took me an embarrassingly long time to figure out that the guy was you."

Ben leans forward, balancing on the balls of his feet, like he might actually be sick.

"There I was, pregnant with your baby, watching you make out with some other woman. I was angry...I was *devastated*. I went back to my apartment and cried myself to sleep." Even now, five years later, I still remember the ache in my chest, how difficult it was to breathe as I lay there that night, alone and scared. "I lost it the next morning," I tell him, tears pricking my eyes. Ben bows his head. I know there's a part of him that wants to run, but he stays. He *stays*.

"I figured that was my chance to get a fresh start without you, so that's what I did."

An immeasurable silence stretches out between us as Ben processes what I just told him. For years I had considered telling him about that day, but I never really saw the point of giving him the possibility of something, only to take it away. Even years later, a part of me wanted to save him that pain.

He's feeling it now though, I know.

"How can you even look at me?" Ben asks roughly, turning his head back in my direction. His eyes are shining with tears.

I stand, and take a step toward him, resting my hand on Ben's back, between his shoulder blades. He flinches away from me, like my touch actually burns him.

"You asked me why I broke up with you," I explain. "But you never asked me what made me stick around so long in the first place."

That must shock him, because his eyes actually meet mine again.

"What?"

"You know how they say that you are the person you are when people aren't looking?" I ask.

"What does that have to do with anything?"

A small, sad smile pulls at my lips. "That wasn't the only time I saw you when you thought I wasn't looking."

"I know I asked for it," he says quietly, "but I don't think I can take hearing about all the other ways I was a fuck up tonight."

"So how about I tell you about the ways that you weren't?"

Ben looks almost hopeful, definitely curious. Incredibly cautious.

"Ask me why I stayed," I tell him again.

It takes him a minute, but he does it.

"Why did you stay?"

"Because you used to go to my grandmother's nursing home and read her poetry on Wednesday afternoons," I tell him.

His eyebrows scrunch together. "How did you-"

"When we would go to the movies," I continue, ignoring his question, "you'd always wear that brown leather jacket I liked, even if it was ninety degrees outside, because you knew I'd get cold in the middle of the movie. You always ordered pizza with the crust a little burnt, because even though you hated it, I loved it that way. You'd wake up at five thirty in the morning—before I even got up—to turn on the towel warmer in your bathroom so I wouldn't be freezing when I got out of the shower."

Ben looks utterly lost right now, eyes wide and searching mine.

"That's the guy it was so difficult for me to give up on," I explain. "And I can look at you because that guy is who you are now. And I'm giving him another chance."

Ben turns toward me, his eyes searching mine before he gives me a soft, tender kiss.

"I'm so sorry," he says, pressing his forehead against mine. "I'll never be able to tell you how sorry I am. For what I did, for who I was."

"Show me, then."

"How," he says eagerly. "Tell me how, and I'll do it."

"You're doing it," I say, smiling. "You care about the things that I care about. You're being supportive, and helpful, and amazing. Be the guy I know you can be. That's how you show me you're sorry."

"I can do that," he says through a smile.

"I know you can. I have a condition, though."

"Anything."

"The past?" I say, sliding my hand across his chest before wrapping my arm around his neck. "It stays right here. If we're going to be together, if we're going to move forward, we have to let it go. No bringing it up in fights, no guilt, no angst. Okay?"

Ben blinks, like he can't believe this is happening. "Okay. I just wanted to apolo-"

I press my finger against his lips. "Clean slate."

He nods. "Clean slate."

Using the arm that's anchored around his neck, I pull myself up and give him a proper kiss. A kiss that's full of promise, and hope.

A kiss that's like a beginning.

CHAPTER
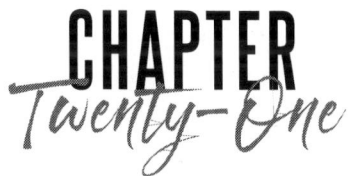
Twenty-One

"**O**h my god, I *love* these," Mia says, as she delicately removes the top of the box full of colorful macarons that I brought her from a fancy French bakery downtown. After she takes a few seconds to survey the delicious inventory, she smiles at me. "You brought all my favorites."

I shift in my chair, as some of the nervous tension I was feeling drains out of me. To be honest, when Mia suggested that the two of us get coffee together the night we met at the Murphy Building benefit, I never thought that I'd actually take her up on the offer, much less be the one who arranged the meeting.

Yet, here we are.

"I'll admit to cheating there," I tell her. "I called Caleb and asked him what you would like."

She tilts the box in my direction. "Share one with me."

Normally I would beg off, but Mia has this friendly warmth to her that makes it difficult to say no.

I reach forward and pull out a pink one, which is rose-flavored, if I remember correctly. I take a small bite, and have to stifle the groan that threatens to come out. We're in public; I can't make noises like that over food, I remind myself.

"So," she says, before pulling a green cookie out of the box. "I'm always up for treats, so please don't think I'm being ungrateful, but what is this for?"

"It's a thank you," I reply.

"What for?"

"For everything you did to help my sister and me. And Ben, too."

She gives me an unassuming smile. "I was just doing my job," she says.

"No," I reply, not wanting her to get away with shrugging this all off as some part of her job description. "Please don't make it sound like less than it was."

She takes a sip of her latte, and nods. "Okay."

"I know we don't know each other very well-"

"*Yet*," she says.

I grin at her. "We don't know each other very well *yet*, but Ben told me how hard you worked trying to decode that flash drive, and some people, they might've given up. You did that for me and Corinne, two people who are strangers to you, and

I owe you the world for that."

"It was nothing," she says.

"It was *everything*. Both to me and to my sister. And to Ben, too. Macarons don't even begin to cover it, but it's a start."

Mia puts the top back on the box of macarons, and pushes it aside, giving her room to lean forward and rest her elbows on the table.

"I don't have any blood relatives left," she explains. "But I know how important family is, and I know that you can build one that means just as much to you as the one you're born into. Being with Caleb has given me the opportunity to build a family. Oliver is part of that, and Ben is, too. Ben might be my boss, but he's my friend, too. If he needs me, I'm there. And he cares about you and your sister, so of course I was willing to do whatever I could to help."

She's right about family, about how your friends can take you in, and give you shelter and comfort and love that you sometimes can't find from the people in your life who are supposed to give you those things. That family can be there for you when the other one falls apart.

I'm just getting to know Mia, and getting reacquainted with Oliver and Caleb, but they've all offered me a network of support over the past few weeks that I thought I'd lost the day my mother and father got arrested.

The realization that I can have that tight knit feeling with a family of my own making gives me a hope for the future that

I didn't think I'd have again.

"Ben told me that he thinks you and I have a lot in common," I say, before wrapping my hands around my warm coffee cup.

"A protective streak a mile wide is the way he put it," Mia replies, laughing.

"Well, if you're going to do something stupid, do it for someone you love, that's my motto."

Mia laughs. "I couldn't agree more."

I want to ask her more about her family, about why she's had to find one in our small group of friends, but we don't know each other well enough for that yet. I want to, though. Anyone who has such a great capacity for caring in her heart that she would do what she did for me after only meeting me a handful of times, and for Corinne, having never met her at all…well, that's the kind of person that I want to have in my corner.

And I want to be in her corner, too.

When I called and asked her to meet, she told me that she didn't have a lot of time this afternoon, so I know she's gonna be going on her way soon.

"Do you think we could meet for coffee again?" I ask. "It'll be nice to talk to you away from the guys."

Mia's whole face brightens.

"I'd really like that," she says. "I'm still new in the city, and even though I've met a bunch of people through work, it'll be nice to have a *friend*, friend. That probably doesn't make any sense." Her face turns kind of red, and she lets out this nervous chuckle.

"It makes perfect sense. You need someone you can talk to without work being the focus of the conversation. Someone you can share things with and not have to look in the eye at the office."

She nods enthusiastically. "Yes, that's exactly what I meant."

"I'd love to be your *friend*, friend. I work for myself, and I tend to spend long hours at my kitchen table, wrapped up in my site."

"A site that I *love*, by the way."

I can't help the short wave of bashfulness that overtakes me. My site is successful and getting bigger by the day, but it still catches me off guard whenever someone talks about how much they like it. It's so fulfilling, putting something out into the world that people enjoy.

"Thank you," I reply. "I get a ton of great samples, and I'm always happy to share."

Her whole face lights up. "Seriously?"

I nod, laughing. "Seriously."

"Next time we meet for coffee, we can take it back to my place, and I'll show you."

"That sounds great."

"If you don't mind," I say, pulling my phone out of my pocket. "Give me your cell number. I'll text you my address, and we can set a date."

Mia takes my phone and happily taps away at the keys.

I smile as I watch her, thinking about how life is full of happy little coincidences. I probably never would've met this woman if I hadn't let Ben back into my life.

Pushing one door open opens so many more. I'm ready to walk through them all.

CHAPTER
Twenty-Two

After everything with Preston Pollard settles down, Ben and I drift into an easy rhythm together. When Stuart and his team complete a full sweep of my place and find nothing amiss, Ben and I start splitting our time between our places.

Some mornings I wake up in Ben's arms in my own bed, and some mornings we wake up together in his.

The two of us are both slammed at work. Development continues on RV-7, keeping Ben and Mia at the office until way past dark most nights. Clothing, jewelry, and accessory designers continue flocking to my site, wanting to take advantage of its growing popularity to get a wider audience for their products.

Felicity and I work together more and more often; we become a pretty good team.

With the overwhelming demand of our jobs, it would be

easy for Ben and I to drift apart, to lose sight of each other, to put our relationship on the back burner.

Somehow, it only brings us closer together. We carve out time in our day to make each other a priority. Sometimes I bring lunch to Ben between meetings, and sometimes he meets me on set at a shoot to share some takeout. Ben sneaks away during his late-night programming sessions for a quickie in his office.

It's not ideal, but it's exciting.

Every night, we manage to find our way back to each other.

We only get the chance to spend one or two full days together a handful of times in the months since we got back together, until Ben and I decide to make it a point to have one day every weekend to ourselves, no interruptions. It takes some doing, but it's worth it.

Sometimes we dress to the nines and go out on a date. Ben is still pretty good at the wooing. Even though he has me, he doesn't stop trying to hold on. Sometimes we stay at home, never leaving the bed, getting lost in each other over and over again.

Tonight, we're in our pajamas, cuddling together as the credits for a movie we just watched together roll across the screen.

"I thought you were kidding when you told me you learned how to lay tile," I tell Ben, because he's just revealed some plans to me about wanting to redo his kitchen floor that took me by surprise.

"Why would I kid about that?"

"I don't know," I reply, laughing. "I thought it was a metaphor or something."

"When have I ever gone that far for a metaphor?" He looks so amused, I just want to kiss the look right off his face.

"It's just that when some rich guy tells you that they took a tile laying class at a hardware store, it's like…I don't know, you assume that it's fiction, or him trying to get in touch with his everyman. A version of a mid-life crisis if you will."

After catching the look on Ben's face when the words "mid-life crisis" come out of my mouth, I make sure to backtrack as quickly as possible. "Not that you're middle-aged. You're not even thirty," I reply, stating the obvious.

"But I *am* some rich guy?" Ben says, laughing, pretending to be offended.

I lean over and playfully kiss his cheek. "You're *my* rich guy."

He squeezes me tightly. "Your rich guy who can actually lay tile and wants your opinion on something."

"My rich guy who's going to lay tile after he finishes rehab on that hand, right?"

The cast is long gone, and Ben is probably tired of me bugging him about keeping up with his physical therapy appointments, but his hands are talented, and I want him in tip-top shape. I'm annoying him, though. The look he gives me tells me as much.

"Ask away," I say lightheartedly, dropping the PT talk. "I'm ready to opine."

"Do you like the slate or the grey for the kitchen?" Ben asks, motioning toward the two different tile samples that are sitting on his coffee table.

"They both look grey to me," I say, snuggling against his chest. His arms are wrapped around me, and I'm warm and comfortable. Perfect.

"This one is more blue." He lifts his bare foot up, tapping on the edge of the tile on the left with his big toe. "The other one is more grey."

"Which is why it's called grey, I guess."

Ben tickles my side a little, and I lean into him to get away from it. Judging by the way he nestles his face into my hair, I'm guessing he doesn't mind that too much.

"I like the slate, I guess."

"Don't sound too enthusiastic about it," he teases.

I shrug. "They just..."

"Don't say they both look grey."

I tilt my head up and kiss his chin. "Okay, I won't. I shouldn't have to point it out, because that's grey on grey, babe."

Ben rolls his eyes. "You're lucky that I love you," he says.

The words just tumble out, and steal all the breath out of me.

It's not the first time I've heard that this time around, but it is the first time that he said it without any explanation. When we first got back together, he let me know that his love for me never went away, so I knew it was there, but this time he's saying it because he just wants me to know.

No agenda, just love.

He catches himself almost instantly, realizes exactly what he's said. His eyes widen for just a moment, like he surprised himself. Then he gives me that look that he has so often, the one that makes me feel precious and safe and like I'm the only woman in the world.

He leans in, tangles his fingers in my hair, and says it again. Right against my lips. Then he kisses me, and puts every single ounce of that emotion into it.

I *feel* it crackling and sparkling all the way down to my toes.

"I am lucky," I say, and Ben looks like he doesn't believe it. That night out on the balcony really rattled him, and it seems like he's still struggling to see the good in himself sometimes.

I feel lucky to be loved by this Ben. He's charming and thoughtful, and he cares about me and my sister. He's everything that I want in a boyfriend, flaws and all.

He's all that I hoped for, and thought I would never have.

"And I love you," I continue, because the feeling is so strong right now that I can't *not* say it. I've been feeling it for a while now, sooner than I thought was wise, given our history.

But that love I feel is filling up every part of my life now:

making me excited to open my eyes in the morning, making me look forward to stolen moments and quiet kisses. That love makes me feel at home here in his arms, and it's only right that I should tell him that.

Ben tugs on my waist, the words spurring on something inside of him, so I lift myself up until I'm straddling his lap.

He reaches up and cradles my face in his hands. He's looking up at me, full of wonder, and I'm beaming back at him like he's the sun.

"Say it again." His voice is completely wrecked. "Please."

I scrub my hand lightly across his stubble, letting the pad of my thumb trace the curve of his lower lip.

"I love you, Ben."

He turns his head, and kisses my palm, his eyelids fluttering shut. He seems completely overcome with emotion, which is something that I so rarely see. It looks good on him.

"You okay?" I ask.

He nods. "Yeah, I just...I didn't think I'd ever hear that again."

I give him a kiss, long, and slow, and deep. "I'm happy to tell you any time you like. But remember our deal?"

Seems like a little love fog has made him completely forget about the fact that I forbade him from ever bringing up the past again. I don't want what's supposed to be an incredible sentiment to get swept away in a sea of self-doubt and deprecation.

"No bringing up the past," he says dutifully, with a gorgeous grin, like he's so proud of himself for remembering.

It's so cute I have to kiss him. Positive reinforcement, and all that.

"Absolutely not."

"Since talk of the past is forbidden, how about I bring up the future?"

My heart skips a beat, just hearing that f-word, but I'm quick to answer, because I don't want him to think that I'm freaking out or anything.

"What about it?" I ask.

"Before I get started with a big project that will take up some of our time together, and probably require you to come with me to the hardware store to pick up things like cement and tile spacers." I groan, but he ignores me. "I wanted to know what you thought about something."

"As long as you're not going to ask me to choose between two grey tiles, I'll tell you anything you want."

He smiles, but it's apprehensive, and he trails his fingers up and down my side, like he's trying to work up the courage to ask me something. I'm pretty sure I know where he's headed, but I'm going to let him get there on his own.

"We haven't spent a night apart since..."

That night on the balcony. I know. "Yeah," I breathe.

"I like that you're the first thing I see in the morning when I wake up," he admits, fingers still trailing across my skin. "And the last thing I see at night."

"I like that too." Nervous Ben Williams is a sight to see, and I can't help but grin, even though he's suffering.

"I was wondering what you think of moving in together. Making the waking up and going to sleep together more of a permanent thing."

"I like permanent things," I tell him, and he visibly relaxes at that. "Where would you like to fall asleep and wake up with me?"

He shrugs. "We could find a new place together. You could move in here, or I could move in with you. Honestly, I really don't care where we are as long as you're with me."

Completely on its own, my mouth lets out this strangled, high pitched noise.

"What?" he asks, smiling.

"You've become such a sap in your old age."

Ben tilts his head up and kisses me. "You like it."

"No," I correct. "I love it."

Truth is, I love my place, but with my work bringing me downtown more often, it would be more convenient to be closer. Ben's neighborhood is great, but his apartment isn't a place I would choose for myself, and I could see the two of us running out of space with all of our stuff.

"What do you think?" he asks, sounding a little anxious, probably because I haven't answered him yet.

"This time around, we're all about the clean slates. So if

we're going to move in together, then I think it should be a new place that we pick out together."

"Yeah?"

I nod. I'm absolutely sure about this. "Yeah."

He picks me up, bumping his shins against the tiles on the coffee table, sending them toppling down to the floor. I hang onto him tight, pressing my body against his.

He kisses me through his smile, and when I lean back to get a look at his face, I say, "What are we doing?"

Even though he's laughing, I can feel him hard and insistent against my thigh. I give my hips a little thrust, which makes him groan.

"There are still a few places we haven't had sex," he tells me matter-of-factly.

"You're supposed to christen the rooms when you first move in."

He takes my earlobe between his teeth, giving it a gentle tug. "It's never too late."

CHAPTER
Twenty-Three

I t takes a while—so long, in fact, that I'm pretty sure our real estate agent is only hanging on for her potential commission—but Ben and I finally find a place in the perfect location. It's a remodeled loft in a lovely old building that's halfway between his office and the studio that Felicity and I like to schedule shoots in.

It feels like home the moment we step inside. It's modern, but not sterile, with room enough for the two of us to have our own spaces if we need them. There's also "room to expand," as the real estate agent so helpfully informed us. Repeatedly. That room to expand comes in the form of two extra bedrooms on the main floor that Ben and I have pointedly avoided talking about, other than deciding that we'd furnish them both as guest rooms.

Furnishing the new place was the first test of our

relationship. Finding pieces that we both like—Ben with his modern taste, and me loving more classic things—was a challenge, but we made it through.

The final step is actually moving, which so far has been a nightmare. I hate it even under the best circumstances, but today we've been dealing with lost boxes, and delayed trucks. The moving company finally got it together, and we're almost, finally done.

The place is littered with boxes, and the movers still have a few more to bring up from the truck. I've been holed up in my office all morning, figuring it was best to get started on something, and being in the loft would keep me far enough from the action on the main level that I wouldn't be in anyone's way.

My back is starting to cramp from the workout I've been putting it through today, so I stand up and stretch. The loft looks out onto the living room below, with floor-to-ceiling windows that usually have a lovely view of downtown.

It's overcast today, and with the lights on inside, the windows are covered with reflections. I'm surprised when I look down and see Ben sitting with Caleb at the dining room table. I had no idea he was coming over, and want to go down and say hello.

It seems like forever since I've seen him, and I wonder if Mia is here, too. I haven't seen her since the last time we met for coffee, which was just before Ben and I went to closing on this place.

I pad down the stairs, across the foyer, and into the dining room. Ben and Caleb are so engrossed in conversation that they don't even notice that I've entered the room. When I get close enough to the table, I can see over Ben's shoulder, and notice that he's holding a ring.

A diamond ring.

A diamond *engagement* ring.

It's both ginormous and classic. Totally huge, but not gaudy.

"That's gorgeous," I say, without even thinking. I didn't mean to intrude on their conversation, and I definitely didn't mean to comment on the ring *out loud*, but it's not like I can take the words back now.

Caleb startles at the sound of my voice so badly that the chair actually moves.

"Marisa," he says, sounding relieved. Like maybe he was expecting someone else.

I walk around the side of the table, and take a seat next to Ben.

"Am I interrupting something?" I ask stupidly. Of course I am; anyone with a working set of eyes can see that.

Ben's looking over at me, and I'm looking at Caleb, who's the one holding the ring now. He has it gently clasped between his index finger and thumb.

When I catch sight of the way that Ben is looking at me,

there's a momentary flutter in my stomach. Just a flash of a thought that maybe I'm living in a world where that ring is meant for me. But the way Caleb is holding it—like it's the most precious thing in the world—makes me realize that the ring is for Mia.

"May I see it?" I ask.

Caleb gives me this dopey smile as he hands the ring over, delicately placing it in the palm of my hand.

It's platinum, with an emerald-cut diamond, and tiny diamonds set all around the band. Simple, but elegant. Just like Mia.

"It's perfect," I tell Caleb, as he lets out a long sigh of relief. "She's going to love it, and she's going to say yes."

"You think?" He looks like he's about to jump out of his skin, like he just wants to chuck whatever plans he's made to go home and ask her already.

"I don't think," I reply with a smile. "I know. She's going to say yes."

"I hope so."

I look over at Ben, who is watching me with an intensity that I can't quite get a read on.

"It belonged to my mother," Caleb says, as I hand the ring back to him.

I know a little bit about Caleb's tragic backstory, and how his parents died. He holds everything he has left of them close, so giving this to Mia is everything. Just because of that, I know how sure he must be that what he has with Mia is forever.

"Your father had amazing taste," I tell him. "You aren't just carrying this around with you, waiting for the right time, are you?"

"No," Caleb replies, shaking his head. "Of course not. I just got it sized, and…"

"Wanted some moral support?" I ask.

Caleb smiles. "Yeah, something like that."

"When are you going to ask her?"

"Tonight," he tells me.

There's a nosy part of me that wants to ask him what he has planned, but that's an incredibly private thing, and I don't want him to read too much into my reaction to whatever it is he'd be willing to tell me.

I'm surprised that Ben's still sitting there quietly. I don't think he's said a single thing since I sat down. I figure that must mean that I walked in on a private conversation, so I decide to give the two of them their space.

"Well," I sigh, as I stand up. "I just thought I'd come down and say hello. I'm going to go back upstairs and finish unpacking."

As I walk around the side of the table, I slide my hand along Ben's broad shoulders. Before I let go, he reaches up and clasps my fingers, giving them a little squeeze.

"I'll come up and help once we're done here," Ben says.

I pat Caleb on the back. "You'll give us a call or send us a text when she says yes, right?"

Caleb beams at me like he's the happiest man in the world, and he hasn't even gotten an answer to his question yet.

"Yes," he replies. "Of course."

"Okay. I guess we'll hear from you later." I give him a playful wink, and then head back upstairs.

I'm shelving the very last of my books on my impeccably organized bookshelf when I hear Ben clearing his throat.

I look back, and he's leaning against the doorframe like some kind of GQ model, looking completely unfair. We've been hauling boxes all day, but somehow he still manages to look like he stepped out of the pages of a magazine with his low-slung jeans and incredibly nice t-shirt that stretches perfectly over his broad chest.

Seeing him like this—relaxed in a place that we own together—gives me the warmest, indescribable feeling in my chest.

"Need any help?" he asks.

I shake my head. He's giving me all the help I need just standing across the room looking like he does.

"I'm almost done here. Is Caleb gone?"

Ben smiles. "Yeah, he's gone. I don't think I've ever seen him move that fast."

I laugh lightly. "It's pretty cute that he wanted to stop by and talk to you before he went and popped the question."

"I won't tell him you said that."

"What?" I ask. "Is there something wrong with being cute. I think *you're* cute. I mean, along with other stuff. But cute is definitely one of them."

If I didn't know better, I'd think Ben was blushing as he smiles down at the floor.

"Sorry you walked in on that. He stopped by at the last minute, after he picked up the ring from being resized. I didn't have time to tell you, and I wasn't sure when you walked up if you thought…"

He trails off nervously, and I want to ease his mind about what my expectations are now.

"If I thought you'd be careless enough to sit at our dining room table holding an engagement ring that you meant to give to me?"

That gets a smile out of him. "Yeah, something like that."

"I didn't think that," I lie. Then I think better of it, because the two of us make it a point to always be honest with each other. "Well, I thought that for a split second. A fraction, just… the tiniest part of a second, however big that is."

That confession is enough to make him push off of the doorframe and stand up straight.

"You did?"

"Well, sure," I say with a shrug. "Any girl who walks into a room and sees her boyfriend holding a ring like that…her mind is going to go places."

"Good places?" His eyebrows are raised, and his hands are shoved in his pockets. He looks so earnest and young that it makes my chest ache.

"Pleasant places," I admit. "Very nice places."

"I'm sorry, I didn't think. I hope you're not disappointed."

"I'm not. I wasn't expecting you to propose to me, Ben," I explain, quickly letting him off the hook for whatever scenario he's convinced himself that I've worked up in my mind.

He crosses the room in three long strides, and wraps is arms around me.

"But if I want to propose to you?"

I smile against his chest, resting my hand right over his erratically beating heart.

"If you want to, then when the time is right you will. Although I'm going to do my best to test your resolve by making you come with me when I go shopping for all new gadgets for our kitchen. If I don't bore you to death first, then you can decide if you want to marry me."

The air between us is charged for a moment, full of the wonderful possibilities that the future might hold for us.

"I don't know," he says, before pressing a kiss against my head. "Nothing is usually boring when I'm with you."

I smile, then tilt my head up and give him a kiss.

With my office all set up and settled, I decide to tackle the living room next. I pick a box completely by random, which turns out to be a bunch of old pictures that I've had packed away since before I moved into my old place.

It's nice to go through some of the memories. There are pictures of Ben and me from when we were in college, ones that I figure are safe to bring out now that we've started a completely new life together. There are photos of me with other friends I made throughout college, and some with people I met after.

About halfway through my walk down memory lane, I come across a picture that I had completely forgot existed.

It's in an ornate gold frame, the kinds that my mother loved to decorate the house with, but were too gaudy for my simple tastes. Inside is a photo that was taken when Corinne and I were still kids. Corinne is in a short sailor dress, smiling with a huge gap where her two front teeth were missing at the time.

My mom's hands are on Corinne's shoulders, and I'm hanging off of my dad's back, my arms draped over his shoulders as he holds me up by my hands. I'm resting my head in the crook of his neck, and we're smiling just like any other family.

I wonder how many crimes Mom and Dad had committed at that point.

I stare at the picture for a long time. It's difficult for me to take my eyes off of it. It's a good memory tainted by the terrible things Mom and Dad have done since, and it feels like a lifetime ago.

Sometimes it's difficult to reconcile how quickly things can change. You can go from friends to enemies in a second, lovers to exes in no time at all. One day you can be a family, and the next day you're not.

"Hey," Ben says, pulling me out of my thoughts as he sits down next to me.

He smells clean, like he just got out of the shower, and he's wearing these sweatpants that somehow manage to not leave much to the imagination.

I turn the frame over, even though I know that Ben has seen what I was looking at. I only ever talk about my parents with Corinne; it's a subject that Ben and I seem to avoid at all costs. I'm sure he doesn't want to do anything to set me off, and I don't ever want to talk about them anyway.

They're still awaiting trial as far as I know, and that's about the extent of my knowledge of them. My lawyer updates me every once and a while, when we go in for a meeting about the legalities of my company. Other than that, I studiously avoid reading anything about them at all. They call occasionally, but I've since blocked their number. They're not really in the news anymore, but that will probably change when they go to trial.

"Hey." Ben has his hands planted behind him on the hardwood floor, and he's leaning back, his legs crossed at the ankles.

"Can I ask you a question?"

I nod. "Yes," I whisper.

"You sure? It might be taboo." Ben's eyebrows are all scrunched together, like they always are when he's thinking hard about something. And his lips are pursed, too.

"We live together now, Ben. Our underwear goes in the same laundry basket. I don't think there's such a thing as taboo between us now."

Ben laughs, and his whole demeanor changes. "No, I guess there isn't."

"So ask away."

"Do you think you'll ever make up with them?" He nods toward the overturned frame sitting on my lap.

It's something that I think about a lot, late at night when I'm tossing and turning and can't seem to get comfortable lying in Ben's arms. I don't know that I can ever trust them again, and that's an important part of a relationship with anyone, whether they're a parent or just a friend.

Being with Ben has taught me that I have a huge capacity for forgiveness, which means that no door is ever truly closed with me. Or, it isn't where my parents are concerned. Not yet, at least.

"I'm not sure," I admit. "Right now? No, I don't think so. A few years from now? Who knows. I can't shut the door on it completely. It's difficult for me to do that."

Ben gives me a wistful smile. "I'm thankful for that every day."

I lean over and kiss him. "I'm thankful for that, too. I'd be missing out on a lot, otherwise."

"That's true," he says, slinging his arm around my shoulder. "Can you believe we own a house now?"

"Our names are on the deed like a couple of grown-ups," I tease.

"And it's our first night here, you know." Ben gives me a long, slow, lust-driven kiss.

He reaches up and starts unbuttoning my shirt with one hand. I look down at how nimble his fingers are. "Bless physical therapy."

We both laugh, but mine quickly dies down when he slides his hand beneath the placket, and cups my breast. I sling my leg over his thighs, and straddle him, tilting my head to the right to give him more room to work his mouth across my neck.

His raspy stubble scrapes my tender skin, and I rock against him, all hard and insistent, right where I want him. I reach down and cup him through his sweatpants, picking up the pace as he thrusts up into my hand.

With all the buttons undone, Ben pushes my shirt off my shoulder, and lowers his mouth to my nipple, taking one between his teeth, and then moving on to the other.

I slip my hand beneath the waistband of Ben's sweatpants, sliding my hand up and down his erection. His kisses become less focused as he loses himself in sensation, and he surprises me when he reaches back and lifts his shirt up over his head.

Gently clasping my wrists, he brings my arms back to wrap around his neck, then his hands slide down along my spine, pulling me closer to him until my breasts are pressed against his chest. Ben's hands guide my hips, giving us both the friction we both want so desperately.

When I can't take it anymore, I reach over for the condom I noticed laying right next to his hip.

I pick it up, tapping the edge on my bottom lip.

"You planned this," I tease, carefully ripping the packet open.

"Oh, I hoped for it," Ben says, before leaning down and licking a stripe along the underside of my breast. "You chastised me for not christening all the rooms in my old place until I was ready to move out. I wanted to do things right this time."

"Ah," I say, grinding down on him until his eyelids flutter shut. "Is this the sexual version of carrying me across the threshold?"

"I also carried you across the threshold. But yes."

He rolls his tongue over my nipple, and I temporarily lose my train of thought. Then I remember the condom in my hand, and the ache between my legs that only Ben can soothe.

"Lose the pants," I say.

Ben tilts his head back and laughs, then does exactly what I asked. I waste no time getting naked too, and Ben's in such a hurry that he takes the condom from me, foregoing all the foreplay of rolling it on that we usually engage in, preferring instead to get down to business.

I lift myself up on my knees, then sink down onto him. It's perfect, it's amazing, it's everything it's always been between the two of us.

We kiss as our bodies rock against each other. His hands never stop moving, like they're trying to memorize every inch of me by touch alone. His grip eventually settles on my hips, and I let him guide my movements as I stop thinking and *feel*.

It's carefree and tender and slow in a way that sex typically isn't between us. This is more about just being together than finding a release, although my clit is grinding against him in ways that start making me feel more than a little frantic.

Ben senses that, and reaches down between us, my orgasm hitting me fast and hard as I hold onto him for dear life, riding out my pleasure. Ben follows, his body stiffening with a long, low groan.

After, we kiss and hold each other, clinging to the bliss for as long as we can.

"Are you tired?" Ben asks.

"Of unpacking? Yes. Of this? No."

Ben kisses me, smiling against my lips. "Good. We have a lot more area to cover."

CHAPTER
Twenty-Four

"**Y**ou can cry if you want to," Ben says, his lips brushing against the shell of my ear. The teasing lilt in his voice is the only thing that's keeping the tears from falling. "She's all grown up and leaving you."

Ben is standing behind me, his arms wrapped around my waist, my back pressed against his chest. We're standing in the corner of Ben and Caleb's restaurant—which has been closed for the party—celebrating Corinne's college graduation.

The place has mostly cleared out. It's late, and the only people left are the ones nearest and dearest to her, and despite the hour, she's still gracious, happily accepting congratulations.

She's talking to Felicity now, probably finalizing their plans for tomorrow, when Corinne's leaving to take a job on a completely different continent. Felicity, good friend that she is, is going to go with her for a week or so, just to help her get acclimated to life in London.

I'm happy for my sister; she wanted that job desperately, but I'm sad at the realization that the two of us won't be in the same time zone for at least the immediate future, if not forever.

"I can hear you thinking," Ben says, giving my hands a squeeze.

"Oh yeah?"

"Mmm," he says, his voice all rumbly. "It's her first job; she probably won't stay there forever."

This is true, and something that I've told myself probably a thousand times since she called and gave me the news.

"I'm happy for her," I tell Ben. "Just sad for me."

"I'll keep you company."

That makes me smile. It's not the same at all, but…it makes me smile. "I love your company. And I love you."

Ben hums happily, and presses a kiss to my temple. "I worked up some proprietary video messaging software and put it on all of your mobile devices. One click and you'll be able to talk to each other."

"How is that different than what we have now?"

I can feel Ben's smile against my cheek. "You'll see."

"Thank you," I whisper.

"You're welcome. I've got to go talk to Oliver about something, 'kay?"

I nod, and give him a kiss. I watch him walk over to Oliver, who's looking all lovelorn like he usually does in Felicity's presence. I'm going to have to do something about that.

"We're going to have to take care of that," Mia says.

"Hey! Take care of what?"

"That self-deprecating idiot over there who thinks he's not good enough for Felicity," Mia says, tilting her champagne flute in Oliver's direction.

"We definitely need to help that along."

"Great party. Thanks for having me," Mia says.

I smile at her. "Of course. You and Caleb are family."

Mia beams at that. "Guess you're going to be making a lot more trips to London now."

I nod, laughing. "I guess so. Have you ever been?"

Mia shakes her head. "Nope. Someday."

"We should go together," I offer. "Or maybe that's a stop Caleb has planned for your honeymoon."

"Maybe," Mia replies, looking down at the engagement ring on her finger.

I can't help but stare at the way the light glints off of the diamond.

"Speaking of that, I'm going to need some help finding a dress. I hired a planner, but...I don't know, I feel like finding the dress should be more of a personal thing. I want to go out shopping with friends, and try on some truly hideous dresses before finding 'the one.'"

"You know I'm your girl."

"Think we could get together soon and see what's out there?"

I nod enthusiastically. "Absolutely. I know quite a few places we could go. Both for the 'truly hideous,' and for 'the one.'"

"Well," Mia says, taking a sip of her champagne. "It seems like someone's pretty anxious to talk to you, so…I'll call you?"

"Yeah. Looking forward to it," I say with a smile.

Not even a second after Mia walks away, Corinne wraps me in the kind of hug that crushes you in the most amazing way.

"I'm so proud of you," I tell her, pressing a kiss against her hair.

"And I'm proud of you, too."

"You never let *anything* stop you from following your dreams, and look where that got you. London. What am I going to do with you in London? The time difference. Ugh."

Corinne laughs. "We'll figure something out. We always do."

That's the truth if I've ever heard it.

"You're still leaving tomorrow?" I ask, giving her a cartoonish pout.

"I've got to. I only have a week before I start my new job, and I need to get settled into my apartment."

"Do you need anything?" I ask. I have my checkbook ready if she needs it, even though she's already turned down my money once.

"No, I'm good. Promise."

"Ben gave you money, didn't he?" I ask.

She smiles sheepishly. "He did. And he refused to let me refuse it. He told me a really lovely story about a similar gift his parents gave him when he graduated, and…"

"I know," I say softly, feeling a newfound rush of love for Ben. He's standing over on the other side of the room, and when he looks at me, I can tell that he knows what Corinne just told me. "I know the story."

"So you're not mad?"

My eyebrows scrunch together. "No, of course not."

"Thank you for the party," Corinne says, probably desperate to change the subject.

"You're welcome. I hope it was everything you wanted."

She grins at me, knowing what I'm trying to say without saying it. That I want to know if it was enough, that she's happy even though our parents weren't welcome.

"Everyone that I wanted to be here is here," she assures me.

"Good."

Ben walks over to us, and he gives Corinne a quick kiss on the cheek. "You had quite the haul, graduate," he says, nodding toward the table of gifts. "Mostly envelopes, which is the best, right?"

Corinne giggles, and returns Ben's high five. "The absolute best."

"I'm going to take that stuff out to the car." He leans in and gives me a soft, chase kiss. "I'll see you two in a bit."

As Ben walks away, Corinne is grinning bright as the sun.

"What?" I ask.

She shrugs. "Never thought I'd see that again. It's nice, seeing you this happy."

I don't even know if happy is the right word to describe what I am.

"C'mon," I say hooking my arm through hers. "I have a bunch of your favorite movies at home, and your favorite snacks. We're going to have one last slumber party."

Corinne groans, but it's good natured. "I have to be up at five to get to the airport on time."

"Well," I say lightly. "I can definitely make sure you stay up until then."

Corinne glares at me.

"You have time to sleep on the plane, but not a lot of time left to spend with your sister. Say goodbye to your guests so you can go to your next party."

Corinne gives me an indulgent smile. "Okay."

CHAPTER
Twenty-Five

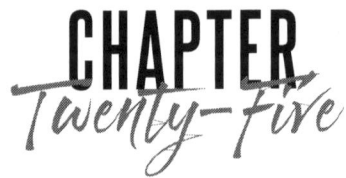

"How dirty do you think that water is?" I ask. "I mean, there's *dirt* dirty, and then there's biologically hazardous dirty, you know? I can't figure out which one we're dealing with here."

One we're dealing with here."

Ben closes his eyes with a long, tortured sigh. "That's what you're thinking about right now?"

I can see how that would be distressing, given the whole romantic atmosphere he seems to be setting with this late afternoon date of sorts.

"There was a train of thought that led me to this station, no worries."

Ben squeezes my shoulder as we walk across Bow Bridge, pulling me closer against his side. This part of Central Park is blessedly uncrowded considering how beautiful the day turned out to be.

"Why don't you take me for a ride on that train?"

"Well," I say, sliding my arm across his back to wrap around his waist, "I was thinking about what a nice walk this is, and how much I love this part of the park."

"Mmm-hmm." He kisses the top of my head.

"And I know how much you love this bridge, and I was thinking about how nice it would be if you kissed me right over there." I point to a place about ten feet away, where the bridge starts curving down. It's as romantic a spot as it can be in a public place like this, with the backdrop of the bright green trees and the flowers. It sets a mood.

"That sounds nice. I'm really concerned about how you got from kissing to toxic water, though."

"Well, I'm trying to explain that."

Ben smiles. "Go on."

"You know how sometimes you like to lean in? Press your body all up against mine so there isn't any space between us?"

"You like it when I do that," he reminds me.

"Mmm. Very much."

"Okay, so…"

"So, I was thinking about what would happen if you kissed me, and leaned in, and maybe I lost my balance and toppled into the water. I would pull you in with me, of course."

Ben laughs. "So, you pictured me kissing you, but not doing it correctly. That's not really making me feel any better here."

"No!" I cry quickly, worried about the directions his thoughts would take. "It was more of a worst-case scenario kind of thing. Like one of those domino trails that people set up and then knock down, but with thoughts instead of dominoes. You always kiss me correctly. I was basically considering what it would be like if we were living in a rom-com."

"You think this is rom-com-y?"

I shrug. "Well, a little. In the best way. It's the kind of perfect date that you dream about, but that rarely happens, you know?"

"I'm glad you think this is perfect. I was hoping you would."

I've been running my mouth so much that I didn't even notice Ben walking us over toward the railing, and pressing my back against it. Wow, it's way too sturdy for me to ever topple over, and I'm nowhere near tall enough.

Still, he's going to kiss me, and I'm not going to complain about that.

I clap my hand against the cement railing, before wrapping both of my arms around his waist, pulling him close so tightly that I think maybe it might be difficult for him to breathe. If it is, he doesn't say anything.

"Wow, you're good."

"Yeah?"

He's *leaning*, and… "Yeah. Really good."

"I can be better." His lips are so close that I can feel his words.

212

I grip the fabric of his shirt between my fingers and give it a little pull, until Ben is kissing me senseless.

"How's that?"

"It's better than finding out how dirty that water is, that's for sure."

Ben leans in and kisses me again, and I chase his lips with mine when he pulls away, not wanting any of this to end.

"Why are we stopping?" I pout.

"We've got another stop to make." He reaches out and takes my hand, sliding his fingers in between mine.

"We do?"

"Yep." He looks down at his watch. "And we're cutting it close, so come on."

"Where are we going?"

Ben winks at me. "It's a surprise."

Even though Ben has his driver let us out of the limo about a block too early, I know where we're going even before we get there. Ben knows that I know, there's no way that he doesn't. But I don't say anything, just let him hold my hand and lead me through the crowd of people flooding the sidewalks.

His thumb runs back and forth over my knuckles, and it's a warm, calming thing. My heart is going a mile a minute, but it's not nerves, it's anticipation. I hadn't really caught on when he suggested that we have a late lunch in the park, and then took me for a walk across Bow Bridge. It wasn't until he suggested that there was another stop to make that I realized he was recreating our first date.

I am completely, without a doubt, one-hundred-percent certain: Ben is going to ask me to marry him.

I am completely, without a doubt, one-hundred percent certain: I am going to say yes.

It's actually difficult for me not to tug on his hand, stop him in the middle of the crowd, throw my arms around him and whisper "yes" against his lips until the two of us are laughing in each other's arms.

When I was growing up, I always wondered how people knew when they were ready to commit their whole life to another person. It seemed so big, so momentous, so scary.

Now, I understand.

The building blocks of a relationship foundation come together before you even realize that they're forming anything at all. It's in the way he remembers that I was scared of stuffed animals when I was little, and the way I remember that his first word was "foot."

It's in the way he knows that pressing his hand against the small of my back will relieve all the tension coiled up in my muscles after a long, stressful day at work. It's in the way I can tell that he's feeling a little melancholy about the past when he disappears out onto the balcony early Sunday mornings. It's the way I know that a soft kiss and a whispered "I love you" will drag him out of it.

We know we're ready because of the tiny things, the little bits of knowledge that we gradually stack into a forever. When you look at what you've built together, you think, "This is where I belong."

I belong with Ben. I want to share my home and my life with him. I want to have children with him, and learn from our parents' mistakes. I want a little piece of him and me to go out into the world and raise all kinds of hell.

So when the scaffolding on the outside of the Murphy Building comes into view, I'm ready to jump out of my skin. When we finally walk up the steps onto the promenade in front of the building and clear the traffic on the sidewalk, Ben slows his stride and looks over at me.

He's wearing this soft smile, and his eyes are bright and happy. I'm pretty sure I'm looking at him the same way. He knows that I know what's going on, but he doesn't try to rush or get on with it.

He takes his time, pulling my hand up to his lips and pressing a kiss on the back of it.

"C'mon," he says, walking over toward the street musician who has his violin cradled between his shoulder and chin.

"Is that the same guy?"

Ben laughs, and shakes his head. "I'm good, but I'm not that good."

"Yeah," I say, squeezing his fingers. "You're good."

The two of us stand together, looking up at the building that brought us together twice now. I haven't been on the restoration board for nearly a year, but one of the remaining members is nice enough to forward me updates. The project is moving along quickly, and they're expecting to have the project finished by the spring.

"They're repairing the cracks," Ben says, his gaze switching from the building over to me.

"Just like we did," I say.

Ben smiles, and it's the most beautiful thing I've ever seen. "Yeah, just like we did."

"You went pretty far for this metaphor," I tease.

He presses his lips together, and looks down at the ground. "I suppose I did. It's okay to do that on a special occasion."

A rush of heat floods through my body, and every single nerve in my body is buzzing. I don't know how I'm not vibrating with it, honestly.

"This is a special occasion?"

He gives me this look of affectionate exasperation.

"You know it is."

I do know that.

"Dance with me?" He takes a step back, our arms stretched out between us, our fingers knit together. He looks just like he did that first night. We're standing the same way, too.

I bite my lip and nod. "Okay."

His grin lights up his face, and the music starts playing as he holds me close. I rest my head on his chest, and I think it's probably the safest and happiest I've felt in a long time.

We move slowly to the rhythm of the song, which of course is the same one that was playing that day. I wonder if Ben found out the name of it, or if he hummed a few bars of it to this guy, and he just happened to know the song Ben wanted him to play.

I suppose that doesn't matter. I stop wondering when I feel Ben's lips brush my forehead, anyway.

"Your hair was up in a ponytail," he says, his voice low, loud enough so that only I can hear him. "You were wearing a purple sweater over a white shirt, because you had spilled coffee that morning and didn't want anyone to see it."

I let out a surprised laugh. How did he remember that?

"I saw you standing on a stool in the Philosophy section, stretching up to reach a high shelf, and I completely forgot what I was looking for the second I laid eyes on you."

I feel tears prick at the back of my eyes, and I cling to him tightly, never wanting this to end, never wanting to let go.

"I reached up and pulled the book down for you, and you said, 'I don't know why I'm gonna bother reading this anyway, it's probably bullshit.'"

We both laugh at the memory.

"It was bullshit," I say, smiling.

"I wanted to kiss you right then and there. And later that night, while we were dancing right here, you let me."

217

"It was a great kiss," I remind him. Toe-curling, mind-numbing. The kind that you read about in romance novels.

"If I hadn't been such an idiot, I would've realized that night that you were it for me, Marisa. I wouldn't have wasted five years not loving you the way that I should."

I take a deep breath, not really wanting him to beat himself up over this anymore, but maybe remembering isn't such a bad thing.

"I don't think those five years were a waste," I tell him, sliding my hand across his chest. "It got us here, didn't it?"

"Sometimes I can't believe we're here," he says with a laugh. "We are, against all odds. And this is exactly where I want to be."

I smile up at him, then stretch on my tiptoes and kiss him. It's slow and deep and probably a little too much for polite company, but I don't care. I'm going to spend the rest of my life with this man, and I want that to start as soon as possible.

He pulls away, grinning like a complete goof, and loosely takes both of my hands in his before he drops down on one knee.

Ben presses kisses to my fingers, and I think he reaches into his pocket and pulls out a ring. I don't know what it looks like, and right now I don't care. I can't look away from him in this moment.

This moment is perfect, and I don't even know what he can possibly say, other than...

"Marry me." His eyes are shining with tears, and his grin is a little shaky, and everything we've been through is nothing, *nothing* compared to this.

"Yes," I say with a laugh.

Ben slides the ring on my finger. I can't even get a good look at it through my happy tears; all I know is that it's gorgeous, and it feels so right on my finger.

"Yeah?" he says as he stands, like he can't believe it.

"Yes. Yes!"

Ben laughs as I help pull him up, and I think there might be applause around us, but I don't care, because all I want to do is kiss this man and never, ever stop.

"We should get married here," he says when we finally pull away.

"Planning already?" I tease.

He nods, wrapping his arm around me.

"For a while now, actually."

My knees kinda of give out on me a little, but Ben is there to keep me upright. He walks over and slips the violinist some cash, then thanks him. He calls out a congratulations to us as we walk across the promenade, back to the waiting limo.

"Where are we going now?" I ask.

Ben turns and smirks at me. "Home, to celebrate."

"We've pretty much christened all the surfaces," I tease.

"We'll do it a second time. That seems to work out pretty well for us."

I stop him in the middle of foot traffic for a kiss, I don't even care.

"It sure does."

About the Author

Cassie Cross is a Maryland native and a romantic at heart, who lives outside of Baltimore with her two dogs and a closet full of shoes. Cassie's fondness for swoon-worthy men and strong women are the inspiration for most of her stories, and when she's not busy writing a book, you'll probably find her eating takeout and indulging in her love of 80's sitcoms.

Cassie loves hearing from her readers, so please follow her on Twitter (@ CrossWrites) or leave a review for this book on the site you purchased it from. Thank you!

21587274R00128

Printed in Great Britain
by Amazon